Heart of Christmas

The Coleman Series

Katie Winters

Chapter One

With a sharp blast of December wind against her back, Estelle Coleman entered the revolving front door of the James Hotel in Midtown, Manhattan, her black peacoat whipping around her and her hair peppered with snow. The foyer was warm and inviting, with flames licking the stones in the fireplace and Christmas music sprinkling in from an invisible speaker system. After the five-hour drive from Hyannias Port, she'd made it. It was nearly time for the next step in her writing career: a book launch that would catapult her writing sales into the stratosphere. She'd hardly slept a wink last night in anticipation.

The hotelier behind the mahogany front desk, a woman in a purple vest with a name tag that read "Shonda," smiled and said, "Good afternoon, Mrs. Coleman. We're so pleased to host you." Estelle's footsteps hiccupped with surprise. In New York City, a place of eight million people, she hadn't expected to be greeted by name. Shonda now placed a bottle of champagne, three flute glasses, and a bouquet of flowers on the counter and clasped her hands. "I've read eight of your books so far. I wept all the way through *A Bride's Reverie*." Her cheeks were pink as she added in a whisper, "We're not supposed to gush over our guests. It's company policy to treat everyone the same. I hope you don't mind that I'm not."

Estelle dropped her nose toward the bouquet, closed her eyes, and inhaled the soft peonies and lilies. She wasn't accustomed to meeting fans, not like this. She felt like a celebrity. But she couldn't be, could she? She was just Estelle Coleman. She was just a wife and mother from Nantucket Island.

"Shonda, I can't thank you enough." On instinct, Estelle reached into her purse, grabbed a copy of her most recent book, *A Bright Christmas*, and placed it delicately on the counter between them.

Shonda's smile widened. "Wow! It's only been out for a day! May I?"

Estelle nodded as Shonda picked up the book, turned it, and gazed at the cover. After a back-and-forth with the publisher, Estelle and her agent had opted for a backdrop of a snow-capped village and a couple walking hand-in-hand alongside glittering water, and it suited the book beautifully.

"It's gorgeous," Shonda breathed. "I already saw a picture of it on Instagram, but it's so much better in person."

"Why don't you have this copy?"

Shonda's eyes widened. "I couldn't."

"I insist."

"I have cash in my wallet. I think?" Shonda scrambled under the counter, maybe hunting for her purse.

"Shonda," Estelle interrupted. "I really want you to have it, okay? It's not every day I meet a fan. I live most of my days locked in my writing office, stuck in my head. It means so much that my stories have spoken to you."

Shonda placed her hand over her heart and continued to grip the book. "Thank you, Estelle." She pressed her lips together and frowned. "I knew I was right about you."

Estelle laughed. "What do you mean?"

Shonda touched the corner of her eye, which glinted with tears, as though the intensity of this moment was too much for her. "I've read so many of your books," she said. "I feel like I know your heart."

The revolving down spun again, and laughter rang out. Estelle's daughters, Hilary and Samantha, appeared, dragging their suitcases out behind them. Hilary's red and Samantha's blonde curls flew out behind them, frizzy with the chill of the early December afternoon. Behind them was the gray frigidity of Manhattan, its yellow taxis blurry as they whipped through a jungle of cement. They were miles from the fresh air of their Nantucket home.

"There you are!" Estelle called.

"Sam was flirting with the valet driver," Hilary said, telling on her older sister as though they were still six and eight.

"I was not. He did give us a deal, though." Sam rolled up alongside her mother and peered down at the book on the counter, smiling to herself.

"Are these your daughters?" Shonda clutched the book with both hands.

"Hilary and Samantha." Estelle beamed. "They're my partners for this frantic week of readings and signings. I'm not a city girl. Never have been."

"Me neither," Sam said. "Hilary's here to get us through."

"You're so lucky to have Estelle as your mother!" Shonda said, reaching for yet another bottle of champagne from the counter behind her and setting it beside the one she'd already offered. It was as though she wanted to throw every conceivable gift Estelle's way.

"I'm sure they don't always think that," Estelle joked, brushing a few flecks of snow from the sleeve of Hilary's powder blue peacoat.

"She gave me one of her books," Shonda said, pressing it across the counter. "I hope you'll sign it?"

"Our mother, the celebrity," Hilary quipped, as Estelle clicked the end of a pen and signed her name in a flourish on the first page. She also added the words: "To Shonda, my first fan in New York City."

The publisher had booked them a suite: one bedroom each for the three of them, plus a kitchenette, a small balcony overlooking the streets that charged, vein-like, across Manhattan, and a luxurious sitting room. Here, Hilary popped a bottle of champagne and filled three flutes with the bubbly liquid.

"We made it!" Hilary cried as she raised her glass.

Estelle collapsed on a mustard couch and selected a glass from the table. "I can't thank you enough for coming with me."

"Are you kidding? Where else would we be!" Sam dropped herself next to Estelle and threw her arm around her shoulder. Estelle had a funny memory of herself with her two girls, maybe forty years ago, when they'd been very small, begging her to read *Little House on the Prairie* or *The Secret Garden* to them aloud before they went to bed. That was the thing about having children: you went through so many textures of time together. You remembered the good times and the bad times and the in-between times.

That past year, Sam had rejuvenated her relationship with Hilary, Charlie, and her father, Roland, which only made Estelle, Hilary, and Sam's together cozier and more emotionally resonant. Sometimes, Estelle thought the three of them could read each other's minds.

This made her think of her own mother, Carrie, whom she'd lost so long ago. Estelle and Carrie had had a symbiosis, a closeness that often led them to finish one another's sentences or help one another with a task without needing to be asked. Carrie hadn't lived long enough to ever get to know Samantha and Hilary, which sometimes hurt so badly that it felt like a knife over Estelle's heart.

"To your new book, Mom," Sam said, raising her glass.

"Yes. To *A Bright Christmas*," Hilary affirmed, her long red hair falling like a curtain as she dropped forward to clink her glass with Sam's and Estelle's.

Sam said this was the first time the publisher was treating Estelle the way she deserved, the first time they recognized just how successful she'd been. "They should have given you book launches and book tours for years," she insisted, although she didn't know anything about the literary world. Still, Sam was right about one thing. Estelle wasn't entirely good at recognizing her own abilities. Despite having decades of success in the world of writing, she still struggled to call herself a "real writer." The fact that Shonda had gushed over her and the publisher had booked this enormous suite didn't quite fit with Estelle's estimation of herself. She told herself to be grateful for all of it and to write down everything that

happened just in case this luck never came her way
again.

Throughout the next hour, Estelle, Hilary, and
Samantha cozied up in the hotel suite, sipping champagne and dreaming aloud about the night ahead. The
book launch was set for seven, with two-hundred atten-
dees. Estelle planned to read chapter five from *A Bright
Christmas*, answer questions during a thirty-minute
Q&A, and spend a good two hours meeting fans and
signing books.

"When you first started writing, did you ever imagine
your career would get this big?" Sam asked, tilting her
head.

Estelle laughed. "The first time I put pen to paper
and wrote a 'novel,' I had no idea what I was doing. I
could hardly imagine finishing a novel, let alone coming
all the way to the big city to launch one." She used air
quotes around the word "novel" because the piece she'd
scrawled across her notebook hadn't had nice descriptions
or character development; she'd hardly known what a
three-act structure was nor how to set a scene. "It was an
inconceivable dream. I guess that's what makes today so
special."

Estelle dressed in a beautiful black dress with a high
collar and a cinched waist. With practiced perfectionism,
she draped herself over the counter to line her lips and
coat them with a dark shade of red. Out in the living
room, Sam and Hilary gushed about one another's outfits
and played a song on a portable speaker, one from their
teenage years that Estelle remembered blasting through
the Coleman House. For a moment, she closed her eyes
and pretended it was thirty years ago, that her teenagers
were safe in their bedrooms, that she was younger, with

more years in front of her than behind her. It wasn't that she wasn't grateful for everything that had already happened. It was just that she wanted to do it again and again: the same kisses with Roland, the same family vacations, and even the same fights— oh, how she loved her life.

The publisher had rented a gorgeous ballroom downtown for the launch of *A Bright Christmas*. At the entrance was a seven-foot-tall cardboard poster of the book cover, along with a table piled high with copies of the book. As Estelle, Hilary, and Sam drew closer, Estelle's agent, Christie, dropped out of the fray of the guests who'd already arrived. Christie had been with Estelle for nearly fifteen years, and Estelle often thought of her as one of her dearest friends. Now, Christie wrapped Estelle in a hug and breathed into her ear, "There she is! The icon, Estelle Coleman."

Estelle laughed. "Everyone has been gushing over me since I got to the city. I don't know what to do with myself."

"Just lean into it," Christie ordered, lacing her arm through Estelle's. "Let's get you situated."

Estelle found herself on stage in front of two-hundred guests, mostly women, who clutched either Estelle's newest book or one of her twelve others to their chests and gossiped in low, excited tones. Estelle's smile felt unnatural and strange, her cheeks stiff with nerves. When Christie gave her a thumb's up, she bent to speak into the microphone. "Good evening, everyone. Thank you for coming out to this little soiree."

Estelle's fans burst to their feet, clapping. Their smiles were enormous. It struck Estelle as completely strange that these stories she'd drawn from within her heart and soul captured these women's attention so completely. *A Bright Christmas*, especially, was taken almost directly from Estelle's life— a formative era that had ultimately pushed her down her writing path. Had it not been for that time of her life, she never would have married Roland, had her three children, or published her first novel.

Sometimes, it terrified Estelle to think about it. If one thing had gone differently, perhaps she would have lived out her days all alone, still dreaming of being a wife, mother, and author.

Estelle cleared her throat and began to read from chapter five. In it, an eighteen-year-old woman named Emma broke up with a man she loved very much. She was keeping something from him, a secret that ripped her apart. The look on her boyfriend's face was the single-most heartbreaking thing she'd seen in her life. But she knew in order to save him, she had to set him free.

As Estelle read, her fans were captivated, their cheeks glistening with tears. Nobody spoke, and Estelle's micro-phoned voice echoed through the hall. When she finished, the fans again burst to their feet and called for her to read more.

The woman who'd organized the event hurried to the opposite end of the stage to speak into another micro-phone. "Thank you to Estelle Coleman for that remark-able, heart-wrenching reading. Now, we'll open up questions to all of you. Raise your hands, and I'll try to keep things organized."

Immediately, a sea of hands burst into the air above the crowd. Estelle laughed as her stomach tightened into knots. She wasn't accustomed to this format, and it terri-fied her to think of what her fans might ask her. Perhaps they'd ask her about a favorite book of theirs, one she'd completed ten years ago. How could she possibly remember every character and every plot point?

The first few questions were standard. A woman in a red blouse asked Estelle what her daily schedule was like, to which Estelle answered, "I wake up around six, have coffee with my husband, and write till around noon. After that, I usually take some time to read, write in my journal, or go for a walk along the beach. As you all know, I live on Nantucket, and I can't get enough of the ocean. Even on the chilliest of days, I have to go for a walk through the sands."

Another question came from a woman older than Estelle, with white, curly hair. "How do you get your inspiration?"

"I wish I could tell you exactly where it all comes from," Estelle said as a blush crawled up her neck. "I feel inspired by just about everything, though. My daughters. My son. My grandchildren." Her heart thudded. "My husband has been my greatest source of love and light, of course. Nearly ever romantic interest has been based on him in some small way, at least." She tapped her copy of *A Bright Christmas* as she added, "Of course, in *A Bright Christmas*, he's even more prominent. I remember Roland so clearly as an eighteen-year-old man. Gosh, I loved him. At first, it was a fiery, all-encompassing teenage love. But it changed, as all love does. I think I love our love now more than any other version of our love."

Several women in the audience applauded again. Perhaps they considered their own romantic love with their husbands; perhaps they remembered their own heart-wrenching origin stories and the easy, comfortable, wonderful love they shared now.

A woman with a very sharp jaw toward the back flailed an arm through the air. "I have a question."

"Let's hear it." Estelle smiled, falling into an easy groove.

The woman stood up. Her eyes glinted menacingly. "What do you think about the recent allegations from Margorie Tomlinson?"

Estelle frowned. Margorie Tomlinson was another prominent harlequin romance writer. Although she didn't know her well, Estelle had met her numerous times at romance writer conferences, where they'd shared a glass of wine and talked about "the industry" and its many pitfalls and wonders. Margorie was a fiery redhead with cerulean eyes and a sharp sense of fashion, and her books were marvelous, heartbreaking, and filled with love and lust.

"I'm sorry?" Estelle asked. "What about Margorie Tomlinson?"

The woman who'd asked the question smiled. "A few hours ago, Margorie Tomlinson posted to her social media account, saying that *A Bright Christmas* is essentially a copy of her Christmas book, *A Christmas Dream.*"

Estelle's lips parted with surprise. Across the crowd, women turned to one another to whisper menacingly, and the mood darkened and intensified. Estelle searched her mind for some memory of *A Christmas Dream*, Margorie's book, but she came up empty.

"I'm sorry," Estelle rasped into the microphone, her voice wavering. "I don't know anything about these allegations. And I've certainly never read *A Christmas Dream?*"

Each of her sentences was raised into a question at the end, proof of her uncertainty. She had read hundreds, if not thousands, of books in her life. Was it possible she'd read *A Christmas Dream?*

"So what's your official statement?" the woman asked.

Estelle's vision blurred as she stuttered into the microphone. "I don't know that I have an official statement. I do know Margorie Tomlinson, of course. We've met several times." She paused and searched the crowd for some sign of Christie, but she couldn't find her. "I always really liked Margorie," Estelle added. "I hope she knows I wouldn't do something like that?"

"Let's take the next question," the moderator instructed, coaxing the crowd forward.

Estelle was breathless as she answered the next several questions: one about her use of backstory, another about her opinions on Artificial Intelligence affecting book sales, and another about whether or not she'd ever had a pet. The questions were wild and varied, and she hardly heard each of her answers. Her head throbbed with Margorie's accusations. Why would she do such a thing?

Chapter Two

1971

For the first time in Nantucket High School history, the Class of 1971 had two valedictorians. Roland Coleman had always been a shoo-in for the position, an A-student with the proud Coleman name and a bright future ahead of him. Old-fashioned Nantucketers who weren't keen on feminism said his girlfriend, Estelle, cheated off of him, copied his homework, and demanded he write her essays. "That's the only reason she's a valedictorian, too," they said. "She couldn't have done it without Roland."

That wasn't true in the slightest. Although she'd been born to a lesser-off family and raised in a little shack near the woods, Estelle had always set her sights on a future of academia, intellectualism, and writing. The real truth was that Estelle had helped Roland with his essays, helping him sharpen his arguments and fine-tune his grammar. When Roland insisted on this, telling Chuck and his friends about Estelle's "incredible aptitude," they didn't always believe him. Estelle tried to tell him it was all right, but Roland usually grew furious.

"What do we care what people think?" Estelle asked him, cupping both of his large hands in hers. "We're out of here soon, baby. These anti-women idiots will be in the rear-view mirror." She kissed his palm and added, "Thank you for standing up for me. But I don't need it."

Roland grimaced with defeat. The fire from the massive beach bonfire became two large flickers on both of his eyes, and he glistened beneath the moon, a six-foot-three sculpture of muscle, a Roman nose, and a strong jaw. When Roland had first asked Estelle out for ice cream four years ago, Estelle hadn't known what to think. Her? Dating Nantucket's brightest and most handsome rising star? Then again, why not? She was just as good as he was: with dark blonde curls down to the small of her back, soft, feminine features, and a well-shaped opinion on just about anything political or literary.

"Hey, Ro! Catch!"

Roland turned quickly and reached out to nab a football from the dark sky. Around them, the class of 1971 celebrated their youth and their freedom. Many women wore bikinis and short shorts, their long, slender legs glistening in the light. Men were shirtless, holding domestic beers. Just that afternoon, they'd been honored as The Class of 1971— and now, they were nothing to one another except ex-classmates. The real world beckoned.

Estelle was eventually dragged back to her girlfriends: Sarah, Jessica, and Rachel. Rachel was secretly pregnant, a fact she'd whispered to Estelle that morning as they'd donned their graduation gowns. "Adulthood is happening faster than I thought it would," she'd said with a wince.

"I can't believe we're out!" Jessica cried, drawing her

arms over Sarah and Estelle's shoulders. "We only have a few months before Estelle leaves us for the big, wide world."

"She's going to conquer it," Jessica said. "Aren't you, Stella?"

Estelle rolled her eyes at the nickname, which Jessica had pushed on her for years. "I don't know about conquering anything."

"The University of Massachusetts won't know what hit it," Sarah affirmed.

"Right? When we visit this autumn, you and Roland will already be king and queen of the campus," Rachel said.

Estelle reached for a domestic beer and popped the tab. She didn't normally drink anything, but something about the spitting flames of the bonfire, her friends' high-pitched excitement, and her love for Roland demanded it.

"Here's to the future." Estelle dropped her head back, closed her eyes, and drank as her girlfriends shouted.

An hour later, Roland and Estelle walked barefoot along the water's edge. Estelle skirted toward the waves to feel the sharp chill of the Nantucket Sound, her heart in her throat. The party was a quarter of a mile behind them, and the bonfire cast a ghoulish glow across the waves.

"I can't believe we're going to leave all this behind," Estelle said, nestling her head against Roland's chest.

"We'll be back," Roland said, his hand upon the crown of her head.

"Will we?" Estelle wasn't so sure. In her mind, they would move from university intellectuals to city intellectuals; they would work as professors; they would attend debates. She planned to publish her first book by the age of twenty-two, after which she would drag Roland around the world with her to meet other writers and her fans. Sometime around then, of course, they would start a family— something Estelle would do with ease despite her urgent demands as a world-renowned writer. Roland wouldn't just help her raise their children; they would have a fifty-percent partnership.

"To visit, maybe," Roland said with a laugh.

"Maybe summertime," Estelle agreed. "For vacation."

Roland and Estelle had romanticized their post-high school plans for years. Roland, who'd frequently fought with his father, Chuck, longed to get away from the power of the Coleman name on Nantucket and carve his own path. Estelle had read too many books over the years and craved an identity that had nothing to do with her parents' poverty and frequent fights. She couldn't believe she was allowed to live her life with Roland by her side. It seemed too good to be true.

Roland drove Estelle back home at two in the morning, which was long after her curfew and, therefore, proof of something. Perhaps it meant they wouldn't pay attention to their parents' rules any longer. Perhaps it meant they were free. However, when Roland pulled up outside Estelle's house, she was surprised to see light pouring out from the front window.

Roland draped his hand over Estelle's cheek and kissed her gently. "Whatever they say to you, remember we're out of here. They can't hurt you."

Estelle nodded, her lower lip quivering. Her parents had never stayed up this late, waiting for her. As she marched up the front walkway and hustled up the porch steps, the front windows shook with her father's voice. As she slid her key into the lock, her mother joined him.

They screamed at one another, spitting with rage. Estelle made a note to herself. She would never, ever fight like that with Roland. They would always approach everything with open-hearted honesty and kindness.

"Look who's home." Estelle's father, Matt, glowered at her as she entered. He was seated in the shadows of the cigarette-reeking living room in his La-Z-Boy, where he ate most of his meals. "The valedictorian graces us with her presence."

"Matt, give it a rest." Estelle's mother, Carrie, sat cross-legged on the living room floor. Her cheeks were stained with tears.

The air was tense with their anger. Estelle closed the door and crossed her arms over her chest. She wanted to ask them what the heck was wrong with them. Why, at every opportunity, did they treat one another like garbage? For not the first time, she wanted to suggest they get a divorce. Clinging to this marriage had only alienated the three of them more.

"Your mother has something to tell you," Matt coughed.

At this, Carrie's face crashed in on itself, and she wept openly.

"That isn't going to change anything," Matt shot. "I keep telling you."

They were officially getting divorced. That had to be it. Estelle filled her lungs with air and raised her chin. As far back as she could remember, she'd fantasized about this moment: when her father finally left, and her mother found the strength to go on without him.

Carrie raised her chin to gaze at Estelle. "Sweetie, I got some bad news today."

"Just tell her," Matt ordered. "Spit it out."

Matt's voice was ragged. Estelle wondered where his cruelty had come from. Was it their poverty? Was it a lack of love as a child?

Carrie forced herself to her feet and walked like a ghost toward Estelle. "Let's go to the kitchen, honey."

As her mother led her away, Estelle glanced back at her father, who stared at the black television, rage etched across his face. Abstractly, she thought about the fact that she and her parents had never been awake this late, all together. Perhaps another family would have stayed up this late to celebrate her status as valedictorian. Perhaps another family would have opened champagne and made a toast.

Carrie put a kettle on the stovetop in the kitchen and placed two teabags in mugs. Estelle sat at the three-person table near the window. An owl in the neighboring forest hooted as it did every night. It had been Estelle's constant soundtrack as she'd studied for finals, a sort of ghost haunting her as she drifted through the night.

And then, another sound joined the owls: it was her father, sobbing in the living room. It chilled Estelle to the bone because she'd never heard him cry.

"Mom?" Estelle's voice was higher than she'd planned for. "What's going on?"

The kettle popped as the heat rose on the stovetop. Carrie rubbed her forehead and stared out into the darkness beyond the window. She and Matt had moved into this little place only a few months before Estelle was born, a time of pinching pennies so they could afford the little shack with two bedrooms, one bathroom, a kitchen, and a living room.

"Mom?" Estelle repeated.

"I have cancer," Carrie said, her eyes still toward the forest outside. "I got the call this morning."

A rush of horror pressed against Estelle's chest. Carrie was only thirty-nine years old— hardly middle-aged. It didn't make any sense.

Because Estelle was so stricken, she stuttered through questions. "What? What are you talking about?" Her chest fluttered with panic.

Carrie sighed. "Lung cancer. I was a smoker for years, as you know."

Estelle did know that. She also knew that her father continued to smoke and exhaled all across the house, in the car, in restaurants. She now imagined her father's cigarette smoke clouding her mother's lungs and poisoning her. She couldn't possibly blame her mother for this, not now, as her father blubbered with sorrow and rage in the next room.

Estelle jumped to her feet. "It's going to be okay," she told herself aloud, pretending she had an authority over the situation.

Carrie blinked back tears and turned to look at Estelle. This close-up, she looked more haggard than Estelle had ever seen her. Perhaps because of her endless hours of studying and celebrating her senior year, Estelle hadn't noticed her mother's symptoms. She had been coughing a bit more lately but always waved her hand and blamed spring allergies. Estelle hadn't thought anything of it.

There was the sound of Matt slamming the bathroom door. His wails echoed.

"Your father doesn't know how we're going to pay for everything," Carrie offered with a soft shrug. "The treatments aren't cheap."

Estelle furrowed her brow. Had they really been fighting about money in a time like this?

"We'll figure it out," Estelle assured her mother. "You're going to get the very best treatment."

But Carrie looked listless. "If you knew how much we had in our bank account, sweetie..." She trailed off and returned her gaze to the window.

"Mom," Estelle blared, sounding angrier than she'd meant to. "This is your health. We're going to get you the very best care, okay?"

Carrie didn't answer. Estelle could do nothing but rush across the kitchen and wrap her arms around her mother, who now seemed so frail, whittling away to the bone. Although Estelle was eighteen, she understood that their lack of funds bred a sense of hopelessness and fear that ultimately manifested into arguments such as these. Matt was terrified to lose his wife, but he was unable to say that aloud. The ecosystem was toxic.

"You should get some sleep, honey," Carrie whispered to Estelle before erupting into a fit of coughing.

On the stovetop, the kettle boiled over, its bubbles popping through the spout. Estelle hurried to remove it, her anxiety spiking. She wasn't sure how she would ever sleep again, not in that house, as Carrie's lungs darkened with sickness and her father howled in the bathroom.

"When is your next doctor's appointment?" Estelle asked quietly.

"Friday."

Estelle set her jaw. "I'll take you. We're going to get through this, Mom. You're not alone."

As she said it, Estelle closed her eyes against another wave of emotion, one that threatened to drown her. She marveled that her father was the only one of them exhibiting such tremendous outrage and pain. Weren't men supposed to be stoic and strong? Weren't they meant to carry the weight of their family's turmoil? Or had all men fooled their wives and daughters into believing their strength, only to drop the ball when they were needed the most?

Estelle swayed in the kitchen and stared at the phone on the wall. Every muscle itched to jump across the room to dial the Coleman House. She imagined Chuck erupting from bed, blaring angrily. She imagined Roland's mother, Margaret, rubbing her eyes with confusion. No. Estelle couldn't wake them or tear through the silence of a beautiful night at the Coleman House. It was better to carry this alone.

Chapter Three

Present Day

H ilary booked a Michelin-star restaurant on the Upper West Side to celebrate Estelle's book launch. The space was small and cozy, with dark red wallpaper, antique tables of darkly stained wood, and candles flickering, casting shadows in the corners. Estelle studied the very small menu as her daughters asked the waiter about the cocktails, none of which cost less than twenty-five dollars. Estelle wasn't accustomed to this high-flying life, but she tried to drum up excitement for it if only to match her daughters' enthusiasm.

"Mom? Do you want to try the jasmine cocktail?" Hilary beamed across the table, drawing Estelle back to earth.

"Um. Sure. That sounds okay." Estelle tugged at her hair and blinked across the tables, marveling at how beautifully Manhattan locals were dressed— in linens and gold jewelry, their hair perfect. As a Nantucketer, her hair was frequently wild and frizzy from the ocean winds.

21

"This place is gorgeous," Hilary said as the waiter left with their drink orders. "I've been dreaming about coming for years. Thanks for giving us a reason, Mom."

Estelle tried to smile.

"What a wonderful launch!" Samantha agreed. "How many books did you sign? Your hand must be cramping."

Estelle studied her hand as though she wasn't sure if it belonged to her or not. She realized she'd hardly said anything since she and her daughters had left the ball-room. She'd stared out the window the entire cab ride to the restaurant, lost in thought.

"I hope you're not thinking too much about what that horrible woman said?" Hilary sounded hesitant.

Hilary and Samantha peered at Estelle nervously. It was just as Estelle had suspected; her daughters could read her mind.

"I just can't understand it," Estelle offered. "I've met Margorie a handful of times. It's not that I counted her as a friend, but I've always respected her work. I've even read four or five of her books."

Hilary and Samantha exchanged worried glances.

"She's probably just jealous," Samantha tried. "I googled her already. It looks like she hasn't released a book in five years."

"And you've released three since then!" Hilary pointed out.

Estelle's stomach was tied into knots. "I hate plagiarism. I've never understood why anyone would stoop so low. For me, writing is so much deeper than copying what other people have done, you know?"

"We know! You would never do that," Sam assured her.

"You're too creative for that," Hilary said.

"And I haven't read that Christmas book," Estelle added. "The one they're saying I copied." She paused as her heart hammered. "I don't think I read it, anyway. There have been so many Christmas books over the years. Maybe they all started to run together?"

"But yours is based on your life," Hilary reminded her. "You couldn't have stolen the story. It's yours."

The waiter returned with three cocktails. Samantha made yet another toast for Estelle's career, and Estelle sipped the jasmine-infused cocktail and heard herself say something about how creative the mixing of ingredients was. Even as she pushed herself through the mechanisms of a night out with her two favorite girls, however, her head throbbed with worry. What if she actually had copied Margorie's book? What if Margorie was in the right?

Back in the hotel that night, Estelle couldn't sleep. She pulled up Margorie's author website, where you could purchase all fifteen of Margorie's romance novels, plus pillows, blankets, coasters, and sweatshirts based on Margorie's books. On the "about" page was a photograph of Margorie next to a window. Her bright red hair caught the sunlight, and she smiled in a secretive way, as though her mind was awash with stories she just couldn't wait to put on the page. Beneath that was a "contact" box. Overwhelmed with the desire to fix this, Estelle began to type into it:

Hello Margorie! It's Estelle Coleman. I wanted to reach out to you...

Estelle stopped herself and deleted the text, her chest thrumming with sorrow. What could she possibly say to Margorie? How could she be reasonable? A part of her wanted to scream at her and tell her just how crazy these accusations were. She would never do this! She respected the art of storytelling far too much.

Estelle retreated from the contact box and purchased *A Christmas Dream* for her e-reader. If she was going to tackle these accusations head-on, she had to do it with all the information at her disposal. That meant actually reading the book Margorie said she'd copied. After it downloaded to her e-reader, she closed her computer and settled in, no longer tired in the least. Had Hilary or Sam known she was still awake, they would have reminded her she had a nine-a.m. radio interview tomorrow, followed by another meet-and-greet with fans. Still, studying Margorie's book seemed more important.

Estelle read the first fifteen percent of Margorie's novel, hunting for similarities. Yes, both Margorie and Estelle's novels were set around Christmas, and yes, both Margorie and Estelle's novels were about young lovers coming back together after months apart. But beyond that, there were many differences. Margorie's book was set in Cape Cod, while Estelle's was set on Nantucket. Margorie's heroine was a painter, while Estelle's heroine was a writer. Further, in Estelle's book, the heroine's mother had cancer, while in Margorie's book, the heroine's father was in a terrible accident that left him paralyzed.

Genuinely confused, Estelle jumped on social media to see what people were saying about the situation. This turned out to be a huge mistake. Already, news of this so-called plagiarism had caught fire, and it was spreading into think-pieces, social media posts, and hashtags that said either #TeamMargorie or #TeamEstelle. Estelle hadn't seen the romance writing community come to life like this in years— and she didn't like being at the center of that attention.

Frustrated, Estelle threw her phone and e-reader to the far end of her California King bed and snapped out the lights. She tried to concentrate on her breath, calming herself into sleep, but her thoughts raced, and her heartbeat thumped. Outside, the city that never slept blared its horns, crying out with an anger that Estelle, who'd never lived anywhere but Nantucket Island, couldn't comprehend. This trip to New York was supposed to be the pinnacle of her career and a celebratory few days with her girls. She hadn't anticipated this. She suddenly, desperately wanted to go home. She wanted Roland to wrap his arms around her and burrow against her. She wanted the strength and peace of her own bed.

The following morning, as Hilary, Sam, and Estelle grabbed coffee and scones from a nearby coffeehouse, Hilary told Estelle the chaos would die off soon.

"Margorie is using your fame as a way to catapult her own books back into the best-seller range," Hilary insisted as Sam nodded furiously beside her. "You know how internet culture goes. People pick a different person to attack every day of the week. By tomorrow, they'll be on to someone else."

"Have you read what they're saying about me?" Estelle asked in a meek voice.

"Just stay offline, Mom," Sam begged. "Don't make us take away your phone."

Estelle tried to laugh, but it died out before it reached her throat. She filled her mouth with piping hot coffee and stared out at a wintry Manhattan, where New Yorkers tightened their scarves around their necks as they ambled toward their destination. Just three more days before she could leave the city, just three more days till she'd see her home again. Maybe by then, the Margorie debacle would blow over.

Estelle met upwards of one thousand fans over the following few days. She gave interviews; she allowed herself to be photographed, and she ate bagels, pizza, Chinese food, and other Michelin-star fare that nearly brought her to her knees with flavor. Hilary and Sam did their best to keep Estelle in good spirits, always ready with a joke or an anecdote and begging Estelle for stories from the past.

"It's crazy that our parents' love story became a top-selling romance novel," Hilary said on their last evening.

"I know! It makes me feel like that much more of a failure," Sam said, referring to her divorce earlier that year.

Estelle swatted her arm. "Derek is a remarkable man. You needed to get out of your marriage to meet him. Remember that."

"I know, Mom," Sam assured her. "Not everyone can live your fairytale."

Estelle laughed. "It wasn't all a fairytale. But you know that. Heck, that's the point of the book. We had to suffer and fight for our love. It was the most painful and most romantic time of my life. And I always knew I wanted to write about it. I just didn't know how until now." She swallowed the lump in her throat and considered adding: *If only I could tell that to Margorie. If only I could explain that this story has lived in my heart for years.*

Sam nodded, her cheeks blotchy and her eyes reverent. They were seated in front of a fireplace at a cozy wine bar in the Lower East Side. Already, Hilary had instructed them of tomorrow's plans: check out at eleven, drive to Hyannis Port, ferry at six, and family dinner at seven. Estelle felt dizzy from the previous few days; she'd hardly slept, and her makeup was doing overtime in terms of keeping the bags under her eyes at-bay.

The following afternoon, the hotel valet driver popped out of Sam's SUV, tossed her the keys with a jangle, and wished them a safe journey. In the passenger seat, Estelle turned on the heat and rubbed her palms together as Hilary spoke into her phone, making a list of "things to do" for herself upon their return. Hilary was a sought-after interior designer for Sotheby's, with artistic skill she'd translated across Estelle and Roland's home. Sam hadn't allowed Hilary to help much with her design of the Jessabelle House— but Sam was stubborn like that.

When the SUV hit the outer edge of New York, Estelle's phone rang with a call from her agent.

"Estelle! Hi. How are you?" Christie sounded frantic, as though she were on her way somewhere and walking too quickly.

"I'm great. The past few days were like a dream," Estelle half-lied. She'd managed to avoid social media for the most part and had thrown herself into book signings and interviews, praying not to hear Margorie Tomlinson's name.

"I'm glad to hear that," Christie said. "Our sales were fantastic." There was the sound of a car horn. "I wanted to call immediately when I heard what's happening."

Estelle's heartbeat blasted in her ears.

"That other writer, Margorie Tomlinson? Her lawyer sent the agency a letter. They're pursuing the plagiarism lawsuit."

Estelle felt as though she'd been punched in the chest.

For a long time, she held her breath, willing time to stop and change course.

"Estelle? Are you still there?" Christie asked.

"I'm here." Estelle's voice was weak. "I'm sorry. I just don't understand. I read part of the book I supposedly copied."

"You bought it?" Christie sounded flabbergasted.

"I just needed to know what it was like." Estelle pressed her palm against her forehead as, in the driver's seat, Sam turned to glare at her mother. Estelle mouthed, "Watch the road," to which Sam rolled her eyes and returned her gaze to the highway.

"Estelle, I need to know," Christie continued, her voice tense. "Did you maybe borrow something of Margorie's story?"

Estelle's heart seized. "What? No!"

"Okay. I believe you." Christie sounded doubtful.

"What are we going to do?" Estelle asked.

"I have to meet with the lawyer," Christie explained. "I'll let you know the next step."

"She doesn't actually have a leg to stand on, does she?" Estelle asked.

Another horn blared through the phone. "I don't know," Christie answered. "Like I said, I'll get back to you."

And just like that, Christie hung up.

Estelle felt dizzy. She pressed her forehead against the chilly window and filled her lungs with air.

"Who was that, Mom?" Sam demanded.

"It was Christie," Estelle breathed. "Margorie is pushing this as far as she can. She insists I stole from her."

"That's insane," Hilary offered from the backseat.

"I feel so sick," Estelle whispered. "I don't know what to do."

Sam and Hilary were quiet. Hilary reached up from the back and touched Estelle's shoulder gently.

"We're here for you," Sam told her quietly. "Whatever happens, we're here."

Sam pulled the SUV into the driveway of the Coleman House at six-forty-five, just fifteen minutes before the start of family dinner. Immediately, Roland stepped out of the house and opened his arms. Estelle leaped out of the car and hurried up the walkway to press her face into the warmth of his chest and heave a sigh. Still muscular and tall, with a wide smile, deep-set dimples, and curly gray and black hair, Roland was the most attractive man she'd ever known. His tremendous capacity for love made him all the more handsome.

"There she is! My famous writer, back home," Roland whispered just loud enough for Estelle to hear.

Estelle raised her chin to peer up at him as a Nantucket wind rocketed around them.

"How was it, bunny?" Roland asked.

"I'll tell you later." Estelle's voice wavered.

Sam hollered from behind: "I have your suitcase, Mom!" The spell between Estelle and Roland was broken, and Roland walked down the driveway to help Hilary with the remaining bags. In the flurry of activity, Sam's two daughters, Rachelle and Darcy, scooped Estelle into a group hug and led her inside, where they showed off the dining room table and the feast Rachelle had spent all day cooking: roasted chicken, sweet potatoes, Brussels sprouts, fresh rolls, and hot apple pie with ice cream.

"She made the ice cream herself, too," Darcy said proudly.

"I couldn't have done any of it without Darcy."

"You had the vision," Darcy reminded her. "I'm just here as your sous."

"It's gorgeous," Estelle said, straining herself not to cry. "I'm starving."

Rachelle and Darcy locked eyes for a moment. Rachelle nodded almost imperceptibly as Darcy asked, "Are you okay, Grandma?"

Estelle sniffled and wiped a rogue tear from her cheek with her sleeve. "I'm just fine, darlings."

"Because we know what online bullying can be like," Rachelle interjected.

Estelle blinked between Rachelle and Darcy, realizing that the drama in the romance writing community had filtered out to the rest of the world. It was like a monster that had doubled its size in just a few days.

"And it's genuinely important to maintain your own sanity," Darcy went on. "You need to stay off social media."

"If you need us to, we can take away your phone," Rachelle offered. "My friends in college had to do that to me for a while."

"You had online bullies?" Estelle asked, suddenly outraged. Who would do such a thing to Rachelle?

Rachelle raised her shoulders. "The culinary world is cut-throat. People were jealous of me, and they tried to take me down."

"But she didn't let them," Darcy said. "She kept her head down and continued to work."

"It's the only real way forward," Rachelle assured her.

Estelle chewed delicately on her lower lip. Would it do any good to tell her granddaughters how deep this had already gone? Lawyers were involved. But it wasn't like

Rachelle and Darcy could do anything, not from the warmth of the Coleman House. Perhaps, now that they were back on Nantucket, the hurricane of the previous few days would finally falter.

"I appreciate you looking out for me," Estelle said warmly, raising up the corners of her mouth into something that probably resembled a smile. "But I'm just a little old lady, and this is just a misunderstanding. I'm sure it'll blow over soon."

Even as she said it, her heart hammered with apprehension. What else had people been saying about her since she'd last looked? Had she grown into a romance novel villain?

Roland's arms wrapped around her lovingly, and he pressed his lips against the back of her neck. Rachelle ushered everyone to the table to eat, drawing Colemans from all corners of the house for the feast. When Estelle turned back into Roland's embrace, she inhaled deeper and closed her eyes.

"I can't tell you how happy I am to be home," she whispered to him. "You should have been with me, you know? The hero of the book was based off of you, after all. You would have been great for book sales."

"Ha." Roland shook his head and smiled. "I'm not the handsome eighteen-year-old I once was, you know."

"I know that." Estelle tilted her head. "You're better than you ever were."

Chapter Four

1971

Since Estelle was very small, she'd made it a priority to help around the house. It was her duty to help her mother, to ensure she didn't run herself ragged while her father wasted his hours in front of the television, smoking cigarettes. After school and on the weekend, Estelle washed dishes, scrubbed kitchen tiles and the toilet basin, vacuumed floors, cleared out ashtrays, and even mowed the lawn, her thin arms shaking as she pushed the machine across the grass. By the time she was thirteen, she'd mastered several recipes to feed her father if she was home alone or both parents if her mother was working late – a task that pleased her. It was clear to her why people wanted to become chefs for a living. Nurturing others was a gorgeous ritual, even if the recipe was something simple, like spaghetti.

Now that Carrie was sick with lung cancer, Estelle found the weight of all household tasks upon her shoulders without her mother's help. One minute, she'd been high school valedictorian and on top of the world, and the very next, she was up to her ears in cleaning supplies, groceries, and bills— so many bills that she'd begun to disassociate. There was absolutely no way her mother could go through cancer treatments and continue to work, which meant Estelle needed to get a job, maybe two. That, on top of household tasks, paying bills, and feeding everyone, became a storm in her mind. She had no idea how she was going to make it all work.

In the proceeding days after her mother's diagnosis, Estelle kept to herself. She mopped the bathroom tirelessly, made sure her mother ate and drank enough fluids, and spoke with the doctor on the phone to get a sense for the next few months' schedule of treatments. Her father, Matt, proceeded to get raging drunk nearly every night; he even missed several shifts, making his way from the bar and back home again at his will. He hadn't told anyone about Carrie's diagnosis, either, which meant that Estelle and Matt were the only people to carry the weight of this horror.

Estelle had kept news of her mother's diagnosis from Roland. When he asked her to go to the beach or meet for dinner, she told him she was needed at home and offered to see him late at night, long after her mother went to bed, and Matt was too drunk to do anything but fall asleep in front of the television. About a week after the diagnosis, Roland's face crumpled with sorrow as he begged her to tell her what was going on. "Are you thinking about breaking up with me?"

The question mystified Estelle. She'd never even considered breaking up with Roland, not since the day he'd asked her to be his girlfriend at age fourteen. It was proof of something, though. She was tearing them apart with her secrecy. And she hated herself for it.

"Baby, I would never break up with you," Estelle whispered, lacing her fingers through his. They were out on a picnic blanket on the beach late at night, and a pregnant moon hovered a little too low over them as though it threatened to drop from the sky and into the ocean. It was chilly, early June, and Estelle was wrapped up in a blanket and Roland's letterman jacket. The tears that dropped from her eyes chilled.

Roland studied her contemplatively, his eyes tormented. "Is it too fast?"

"What do you mean?"

"The apartment. Moving in together. College."

"No! It's not." Estelle shook her head violently. "I want to move in with you. I want to start a life with you. And I know that we'll push each other so much when we're in college."

"I need you," Roland said. "You know I don't know how to write a proper essay."

"That's not true," Estelle said with a laugh.

Roland's smile was serene. "Good. Because Dad and I are making plans to sign the lease."

"Sign away," Estelle urged him. "I'll be there." She swallowed the lump in her throat and urged herself to tell him everything. "It's just that something is going on, Roland. Something I don't know how to handle myself."

"Tell me," Roland said, pressing his face through the darkness so that their noses were nearly touching.

Estelle explained everything she knew thus far: that Carrie had lung cancer, that she couldn't work, and that Estelle needed to take Carrie to her doctors' appointments all summer long, help pay the bills, and keep the house in-line.

"But the doctor told me her treatments should be finished by the end of August," Estelle explained.

Roland's face was stony. "I can't believe you've been dealing with this by yourself."

Estelle raised her shoulders. "Saying it aloud makes it true."

Roland exhaled. "Do you want my father to pull some strings? Maybe we can get her a better doctor?"

"There's only one doctor who handles this kind of thing on Nantucket. Mom needs to stay here on the island for treatment. So that's that," Estelle explained. She wanted to tell Roland that money couldn't solve everything, that Chuck Coleman couldn't whisk in on his flying carpet and make this go away.

"Tell me what you need," Roland said, his voice higher, the way it had been two years ago.

Estelle laughed gently.

"I'm serious," Roland assured her. "I want to help you clean and cook."

"Do you even know how to operate a vacuum?"

Roland swatted her knee gently. "I'm not an idiot, you know. I was valedictorian."

"So was I."

Roland's smile was gentle, and Estelle was awash with certainty that he would be the father of her children one day. But how? That future now seemed an impossibility, far from the current one she was trapped in.

Over the next few weeks, Roland surprised Estelle yet again with his aptitude in the kitchen and with cleaning supplies. Wonderfully, her father had finished nursing his wounds at the bar, and once he left for work, Roland drove over, leaped out of his vehicle, kissed Estelle hello, and got to work. They kept things quiet because her mother was often in her room resting, but they also made things fun— dancing around with the broom, slicing and dicing vegetables in frantic rhythms, and whistling as they cleaned windows. It was a bit like playing house, as though they were warming up for moving in together in a few months.

Three weeks after college graduation, Roland and Chuck drove to Amherst, where the University of Massachusetts was located, to sign the lease for the apartment and investigate the city. Estelle gave Roland a long list of things to investigate, including grocery stores, pizza restaurants, and local bars. Before he left, she gave him a long kiss and made him promise he'd be careful.

That afternoon, Estelle drove her mother to her second treatment for lung cancer. Just as they'd been told it would, chemotherapy had left her staggering, exhausted, and vomiting, and Carrie hardly spoke on the ride to the clinic, presumably because she dreaded it so much.

After Carrie disappeared into a back room for her treatment, Estelle settled into a plastic chair in the lobby with a magazine that she couldn't make sense of. It had been ages since she'd been able to calm her thoughts down enough to read. She promised herself that would go away once she went to Amherst, where she'd dive from one book to another on her quest to fill her mind with the greatest works of English-language fiction. She imagined calling Carrie on the phone from college when they'd laugh about "that silly cancer business." By then, it would be a distant memory.

Estelle helped Carrie back into the car later on, where

Carrie stared dully at her thighs as though her neck was incapable of holding up her head. Estelle rubbed Carrie's neck and upper back, trying to imagine what she could possibly cook Carrie that evening. It had to be something simple, something she could keep down.

Suddenly, Carrie's face scrunched into a tight red ball, and she burst into tears. Estelle's adrenaline spiked.

"Mom! Are you okay? Are you in pain?" She rubbed her mother's shoulders slightly harder, knowing it was futile. The problem was on a cellular level.

Carrie blew her nose with a handkerchief and dragged her eyes toward Estelle's. Hers were dead, gray, and bloodshot. Estelle wondered, for the first time, if this disease might actually kill her. It was a horrible thought, one she immediately tried to delete from her mind.

"Honey, there's something I have to tell you."

Estelle's throat was tight. "Okay?"

Carrie closed her eyes. "Your father left today."

Estelle furrowed her brow. "What do you mean?"

But Carrie was too exhausted to explain. Her shoulders slumped forward, and she sobbed into her handkerchief so that her weak body shook. Estelle's mind raced. Just that morning, she'd made lunch for her father and watched him pick it up as he'd limped out the door, hungover. He'd hardly glanced her way as she'd said, "Love you, Dad. Drive safe."

"How do you know he left?" Estelle demanded.

"He left a note by the bed," Carrie explained.

"What did it say?"

"All you need to know is he isn't coming back."

Estelle sat in stunned silence, staring out the window at the sun-drenched parking lot. All she could think of, right now, was the money her father had brought into the equation— money they so needed. She'd already needed a second job. It was impossible to hold down three.

What she didn't think about was her love for her father. She didn't allow herself to consider the beautiful memories they'd shared when she was a child, how he'd taught her to fish and showed her the best trails through the woods to get to the beach. She didn't think about the fact that, although they were disgusting, the smell of cigarette smoke reminded her of being a child next to her father's chair, reading as the rain pattered on the windowpane.

How could he just leave her like that? How could he leave them both?

Estelle helped Carrie clamber into bed and placed a large pot beside her just in case she got sick. She then retreated to the kitchen to scrub the countertops like her life depended on it. Had her father still been a part of their family, he would have been home by five, but five came and went, and still, their house creaked with emptiness.

At seven, the phone rang. It was Roland.

"Hey, baby!" Roland sounded bright and alive, which was such a contrast to the alienation in Estelle's home. "How are you doing?"

Estelle couldn't burst into tears, not now. Not when Roland sounded so happy. "I'm doing just fine, honey. How are you? How's Amherst?"

"It's a dream. The lease is all signed for, and we've been exploring campus and our new neighborhood. You're going to die when you see this adorable pizza place down the block."

Estelle's heart cracked at the edges. "What's it like?"

"It's owned by this tiny Italian couple. They have to

be in their seventies or eighties," Roland went on. "And they don't just have pizza. They have pasta and fish and every kind of garlic bread you can think of."

Estelle laughed gently into the receiver, even as her eyes filled with tears. "We'll have to start exercising to keep up with all that."

"Baby, come on," Roland said with a laugh.

Estelle knew that Roland thought they were going to be young and free and spirited forever. Much like her father, who'd thought he and Carrie would be fine for the rest of their days. It hadn't turned out like that.

Roland went on. He described campus, explaining that he'd seen where most of the literature rooms were. "And you're going to love the library," he said. "I can already see you in there, driving yourself insane with all your reading."

Estelle laughed again. She couldn't remember the last time she'd picked up a book.

"You sound happy," she said.

"I am! But I'll be even happier when we're here together." He paused. "Listen, Dad wants to go out for another walk. I'll see you tomorrow when we get back, all right?"

"Drive safe," Estelle told him, her voice breaking. "I love you."

As Estelle clamped the phone back into the cradle, her knees wavered beneath her. It all seemed like a terrible joke. And although she couldn't fully admit it, not to herself, she had a sense she would never pack her things and move to Amherst. The future Roland dreamed for them was no more.

And she had to find a way to be okay with that. Somehow.

Chapter Five

Present Day

I t had been a friend's idea to rent the house on Martha's Vineyard. "You need to get out of Wilmington," she'd urged, practically forcing Margorie to press the "Book Now" button and fill her suitcase with a variety of swimsuits, cardigan sweaters, and paperbacks. Now, as Margorie Tomlinson sat on the enclosed porch of the white bungalow overlooking the Vineyard Sound with a mug of coffee steaming in her hands, a croissant on a china plate painted with little blue houses and flowers, and a rush of gray waves surging along the beach, she wasn't sure she ever wanted to leave. She was alone, yes. But she was contented. And that's all a woman of her age could ask for.

It was early December, which meant Margorie had already been on the island for six months. The summer had been quietly electrifying. Just as she'd imagined, she'd donned her one-piece swimsuit daily and swept through the waves, her seventy-year-old muscles tightening and elongating as her strength mounted. She'd read voraciously, everything from the Brontë sisters to the most captivating romances. Three or four times, she'd even considered sitting at the writing desk in the upstairs library, opening up a document, and penning a line or two. This was strange. After all, Margorie hadn't written a single paragraph since the release of her last novel, *A Christmas Dream*. That had been five years ago. She wasn't sure she would ever write again.

Margorie sipped her piping-hot coffee and stretched her arms over her head. A surge of December wind crashed against the bungalow, rattling the windows. She then reached for her computer and pulled up her social media accounts to check on what her romance writer friends were calling "the storm of the century." Sure enough, the storm surged on. #TeamMargorie hashtags mounted, as #TeamEstelle hashtags petered out.

@writermillenial said: it's awful to imagine stealing anyone's ideas. I hope Margorie gets the reparations she deserves. #TeamMargorie

@romancediva334 said: I used to love both Estelle Coleman and Margorie Tomlinson's work, but now, I'm wondering what else Estelle might have stolen from the romance community. #TeamMargorie

@ellenromcom11 said: I just bought all of Margorie's books in solidarity! Down with plagiarism! #TeamMargorie

Margorie's heart lifted. It felt as though she were surrounded by all one thousand of her nearest and dearest friends, and they were all in line to say hello, give her a hug, and assure her everything would be all right. She spent a half-hour responding to social media posts, thanking everyone for their support and explaining the next steps in her legal battle. Her lawyer was in contact with Estelle's lawyer. She wouldn't rest until justice was served.

Margorie closed her computer and walked through the house, across the hardwood floors of the living room, with its shaggy couch, thickly woven rugs, and stone fireplace, through the foyer, where she placed her size-six feet into a pair of boots, donned her coat, a hat, and gloves, and stepped out into the sharp cold. She'd read somewhere that getting five thousand steps before noon was a good way to wake up the nervous system. Because she no longer had a real writing schedule to stick to, she had no reason not to stretch her legs.

Out on the beach were several islanders, all dressed in dramatic layers, with hats tugged over their ears. One young couple had a dog, and they threw a large stick down the beach for him to catch. It got caught with the winter winds and flew wildly, much further than it should have, and the dog scrambled, running like a horse in the Kentucky Derby. When he reached it, he snarled as he wrapped his teeth around it and showed the whites of his eyes. The woman in the couple jumped up and down to congratulate him, her blonde hair flashing.

For a moment, Margorie allowed herself to think about this young couple and the romance they shared. How had they met? Were they engaged yet? Did they want children? A part of her mind began to unravel a story, just from the scene out in front of her, and to imagine where their lives might go from here. This was often how she'd begun her books: people-watching and daydreaming. But just as quickly, she was left with only a gray void where her creativity had once been, the storylines dropping out from under her. She kept walking.

Estelle Coleman's new Christmas book, *A Bright Christmas*, had come to Margorie's attention as recently as October. She'd been on a video call with her agent, who'd decided to press Margorie for details on her next novel, which Margorie had been teasing her with for over a year. "It's not ready to be read," Margorie had told her over and over again. Of course, what her agent didn't know was that Margorie hadn't even started it yet. She didn't even have a seed of an idea.

"Can't you write something like your last book?" her agent had suggested. "*A Christmas Dream* is still one of your bestsellers. And your readership adores cozy holiday romances. I just saw today that Estelle Coleman is releasing a Christmas book in December. The advertisements are everywhere." Margorie's agent adjusted her glasses on the bridge of her nose. "We should be hitting that readership. Those people want more Christmas books! And they miss you, Margorie."

Hearing Estelle Coleman's name had sent a shiver down Margorie's back. She'd forced herself through the rest of the meeting, making dull promises to write a Christmas book by next year, and then googled Estelle's newest output— *A Bright Christmas*. The cover had a backdrop of a cozy, snow-capped village and a couple walking hand-in-hand alongside a glittering ocean.

The site had read: **COMING DECEMBER 2023**: *A Bright Christmas* asks the question: **Is true love better left in the past? Or will this small-**

town couple fight for their love despite the entire world conspiring against them?

Margorie had felt as though her throat was on fire. She read and reread the advertising copy, floating through memories. And then, she'd pulled up her sales page for *A Christmas Dream*, which she'd published back in 2018.

The site read: **Bestselling novelist Margorie Tomlinson presents *A Christmas Dream*: a heart-wrenching tale of two lovers who will stop at nothing to fight for their love despite non-stop obstacles. They know their love is worth it.**

"Huh," Margorie had said aloud, her thoughts sharpening with rage. "Isn't that interesting?"

Based on what Margorie had gleaned from a cursory glance at the blurb, Estelle's book was about a young couple with plans to marry and travel the world together. But the young woman's mother gets very sick, which forces her to break all ties with her boyfriend. "I just want you to live the life you deserve," she tells him. The young woman goes on to be a writer and channels her romantic frustrations into her books. Predictably, after years of going through the world apart, the ex-boyfriend returns at Christmas to fight for their love, yada yada yada. Margorie had read it all before.

Margorie's book, *A Christmas Dream*, was similar in nearly every way. The couple breaks up after the young woman's father is paralyzed and she's needed at home. The young man aches with memories of her and returns to fight for their love. Meanwhile, the young woman has channeled all of her romantic rage and pain into her paintings.

Without asking her agent first, Margorie made the social media post. She hadn't exactly accused Estelle of anything; she'd simply pointed out the similarities between their plots and their advertising copy. It had been like blowing air on some sparks. The internet had run wild with it, pointing fingers and— most wonderfully — purchasing Margorie's books. When her agent had reached out to speak about the "Estelle issue," she'd congratulated her. "This is the windfall we needed."

After her beach walk, Margorie tidied her house, took a shower, and dove into a novel for a while as her hair dried with the crackling warmth of the living room fire. Her agent texted at four-thirty with the news— they'd heard from the lawyer, and it was clear that Estelle's camp was nervous. This electrified Margorie even more. She popped off the couch, hurried upstairs, and donned a navy blue turtleneck and a pair of slacks. It had been ages since she'd eaten out, but she was suddenly famished. She wanted an entire fish with mashed potatoes and plenty of butter. She wanted a glass of white wine.

Margorie drove five minutes to downtown Oaks Bluffs, a quaint and Christmassy town with garlands strung on its mighty oaks, twinkling lights lining shop windows and doors, and a nativity scene next to town hall. Although many of the Martha's Vineyard restaurants shuttered their doors once autumn hit, a select few remained open to serve the Vineyard locals. One of them, Walton's, featured candlelit tables with white tablecloths and oil paintings of angry ocean scenes hanging on every wall. She was seated toward the back, presumably because it was sad for guests to see an older woman dining alone. She didn't want to give too much space for that thought, though. She was celebrating.

As Margorie sipped her glass of wine, waiting for her meal, she allowed herself to remember the first time she'd ever met Estelle Coleman. It had been at a romance novelist convention in Cincinnati, Ohio. At the time, Margorie had been a rockstar in the romance writing world and had been asked to be a guest speaker. Estelle had published maybe two novels at that point, and she'd looked nervous and jittery as she'd introduced herself to the other women. "It's such an honor to meet you," Estelle had said, clasping Margorie's hand. "I've read three of your books, and I find your characterization startlingly beautiful."

At the time, Margorie had wondered: *does this woman know who I am?* But the look in Estelle's eyes told Margorie everything she needed to know. To Estelle, at that moment, Margorie had been a stranger.

Was it possible Estelle had learned who Margorie was? Was that why she'd copied her book? Perhaps. Then again, maybe Estelle had just run out of ideas. It happened.

The host led a man a few years younger than Margorie through the back of the restaurant. He wore thick glasses and a beautiful button-down, and his hair was a chaotic bed of curls. After he ordered a glass of wine and a steak, he bent to retrieve a very thick book from his backpack. Very soon, he dove into it as though the rest of the world didn't exist.

Margorie wasn't sure what it was about this man, nor why the sight of him pulled at her heartstrings. She supposed it touched her to see someone read in public like this. In the five years since her husband's death, she'd hardly gone out to dinner by herself. But this man had solved the problems of fear and boredom alone in a restaurant. It looked so simple.

Margorie watched him intermittently, mesmerized by the way he furrowed his brow right before he turned the page, as though he couldn't wait to find out where the story went. Margorie had once felt similarly about writing; she'd long to know where her own story would take her next.

Maybe it was the wine. Maybe it was the confidence that came with calling your lawyer and telling them to make things right. But suddenly, seemingly without warning, Margorie raised her chin and said, "Excuse me? May I ask what you're reading?"

The man's eyes jumped up toward hers. He looked surprised, as though he'd thought he was alone in the restaurant, although nearly every other table was taken.

"It's Jon Fosse," he explained, raising the book to show the cover. "He just won the Nobel Prize in Literature. I'd never read him, and I had to see what all the fuss was about."

Margorie's heart lifted. This was clearly a man of intellectualism, a rare breed. "I've never read him, either. What do you think so far?"

The man closed his book and placed a large hand on the cover as though he could feel its heartbeat. "It's dreamlike," he said. "Incredibly powerful."

Margorie swallowed the lump in her throat. "From over here, it didn't look like you remembered you were still in a restaurant."

"That's because I wasn't still in a restaurant," the man told her. "I was deeply entrenched in this book." He laughed gently, making fun of himself. "But I appreciate being interrupted. Do you read?"

"Voraciously," Margorie told him. "I love just about everything."

"What's the best book you read this year?"

Margorie thought for a moment, scanning through her fifty-plus-long list of titles. "You know, I loved *Book Lovers* by Emily Henry."

"It was perfect," he agreed with a firm nod.

"You read it?" Margorie's heart opened like a window.

"I try to read everything that comes my way," the man explained. "I own a bookstore here in Oak Bluffs. The White Whale. Maybe you've walked by? It's just a few blocks from here."

Even in the six months since Margorie's "move" to Martha's Vineyard, she'd hardly explored Oak Bluffs, choosing instead to scour the beaches and cliffside and forests for clues on how to cure her aching soul. Over the summertime, the tourists had filled every corner of the town: crying babies and angry fathers and kissing lovers. She hadn't been able to take it.

"I'll have to check it out," Margorie said.

"I'm proud of my selection," he explained, palming the back of his neck. "But I love it when real readers come into the store and remind me of everything I'm missing."

Margorie's head throbbed with curiosity. Was this an invitation to visit him at his store? Well, yes. But he needed customers, especially this late in the season.

"I'm Daniel, by the way," the man said.

"Margorie." A blush crawled up the back of her neck. "I don't usually eat at restaurants by myself."

Daniel laughed, but not in a way that made her feel bad about herself. "Why not?"

"I suppose I'm embarrassed."

"What are you embarrassed about?"

Margorie frowned and glanced around the restaurant. It suddenly occurred to her that nobody else in the entire room gave her any attention at all. As a lonely woman of seventy, she was nobody, just a shadow. Before she could say anything more, the waiter appeared with her fish and mashed potatoes and placed them delicately before her.

"I don't know," Margorie finally answered. "Now I'm embarrassed for being embarrassed."

Daniel returned his book to his backpack and sipped his wine. "I don't suppose you want company?"

Margorie's stomach tightened. "You don't have to do that." She assumed he considered her a charity case, a broken, old woman without a man to care for her.

"We don't even have to talk if you don't want to," Daniel said. "I have my Fosse, and you have your fish."

"Okay. Sure." Margorie sounded breathless as she gestured toward the chair beside her. Had it really been five years since she'd shared a meal with just one other man? Had it really been since Tom's death?

By the time Daniel gathered himself across the table from her, the waiter appeared with his plate. Daniel thanked him and raised his knife and fork nervously. The fourth finger of his left hand had a very soft tan-line around the base, as though he'd once worn a wedding ring. This wasn't so strange. Now that Margorie had finally convinced herself to remove her wedding ring, Margorie had the same tan line.

"To eating alone." Daniel raised his glass of wine, adding, "And seeing where the night takes you."

Margorie clinked her glass with his and felt her soul rise out of her body. A woman three tables away glanced their way, noting them together. What did she think of them? Did they think Daniel was too young for her? Just as soon as the woman looked at her, she turned back to her husband to laugh at something he said. Nobody cared what Margorie did, ate, said, or read. And wasn't that a kind of freedom?

"So, Margorie," Daniel began, slicing through his steak. "Can I ask you the most boring and typical question imaginable?"

"I'll allow it."

"I've told you I run a bookstore," Daniel went on. "What do you do?"

"For a living?" Margorie asked, teasing him. She knew that's what he meant.

"Forgive me. It's boring."

"No. It's not." Margorie tapped her napkin across her lips. "I'm a writer, actually. Romance."

Daniel's eyes were illuminated. "A writer!" He scrunched up his face with thought. "You aren't Margorie Tomlinson, are you?"

Margorie's heartbeat quickened. She was terrified he was going to bring up all that Estelle drama.

"I am."

"I'm embarrassed to say I've never read you before," Daniel said. "But you're popular amongst my regulars. They're always begging me to restock your books."

"What a wonderful compliment." Margorie inhaled sharply. The intensity in Daniel's gaze made it difficult to focus on her food.

"It's only a fact," Daniel assured her, raising his wine to swirl the liquid. "Maybe I could convince you to sign a few copies for the store? My regulars would go wild."

Margorie hadn't made a single friend on Martha's Vineyard in six months, which suited her. As Daniel continued to gaze at her, she scanned her mind for potential ways out of this. Getting close to someone, even in a friendship capacity, was emotionally demanding. But the glint in Daniel's eyes told her he wanted something a little more than friendship.

For the first time since she'd met Tom, Margorie felt a bit like a woman in a romance novel, on the verge of being swept off her feet. As was the cliché, she had to be very careful with her broken heart.

"I'll come by this week," Margorie promised.

"Good," Daniel said. "I'll let you borrow a pen."

Chapter Six

The day after Estelle's return from New York City, she sat Roland down on the enclosed porch with coffee and cut-out Christmas cookies and tried to explain the depths of her current romance writing drama. Roland had just come down from a shower. His hair was tousled, and he wore a big University of Massachusetts sweatshirt, a pair of boxers, and thick socks. As he dug his teeth into the thick layer of icing on a Santa cut-out, his shoulders loosened. After he chewed and swallowed, he said, "You've outdone yourself this year."

Estelle hadn't been able to sleep. Her mind was awash with fears for the future, and she'd stayed up nearly all night and woken up very early, bent on filling her kitchen with Christmas cookies. In her mind, if she had enough treats around the house, her children and grandchildren would make excuses to swing by and eat them, thus never leaving her alone for long. Still, due to her anxiety, the decorating was shoddy on several cut-outs, with sloppy Santa smiles and chaotic buttons on snowmen.

"Roland," Estelle began, cupping her knees. "There's something I need to tell you."

Roland's thick eyebrows pinched together. He set down the cookie and swatted some crumbs from his knee.

"The book I just launched has been accused of plagiarism," Estelle said, her voice wavering. "What I mean is, I've been accused of plagiarism. Me." She tapped her chest nervously.

Roland's cheeks were pale. "That's crazy. You would never do that." His eyes widened. "Remember how angry you were when people accused you of cheating in high school? Nobody believed you could be valedictorian on your own."

Estelle quivered with horror at the very old memory. Somehow, she'd lodged that away.

"I'm sorry to bring that up," Roland added. "I just can't believe this keeps happening to you. You're the most brilliant woman I've ever known. People are jealous. They want what you have."

Estelle closed her eyes. This was what Hilary, Sam, and her granddaughters had echoed over and over again, but the words had begun to sound weak.

Despite what Rachelle and Darcy had urged her to do, Estelle remained logged into social media, and she turned her computer around to show Roland what readers were saying about her.

"Hashtag team Estelle?" Roland stuttered. "What the heck does that mean?"

"They're on my side. And the hashtag Margorie means they're on the side of the woman who's accusing me. Margorie Tomlinson."

Roland's lips parted with surprise. "Margorie Tomlinson?" He said the name with soft, round syllables as though they were precious, religious words. But Roland had never been a romance reader. He couldn't have known who she was.

"I've met her a few times," Estelle explained. "She was really popular when I first started out and gave talks at several romance conferences. Everyone wanted a Margorie Tomlinson novel on their shelves, and romance writers wanted Margorie Tomlinson's sales. Badly."

Roland looked contemplative. "But now, people want your sales."

Estelle sighed and put her computer on the coffee table. "The weird thing is, this feud has pushed both of our sales through the roof. People want to read both of them and argue about whether I stole anything from her or not. But Roland, I bought her e-book the other day, and I don't see any real similarities. Yes, our books are about love, and yes, they're about Christmas. But the buck stops there."

Roland wrapped Estelle's hands with both of his. "This is going to blow over," he assured her. "I promise you that."

But Roland didn't understand the pettiness that so often came with writing communities. When a feud like this caught wind, it burned brightly and wildly for as long as the readers and involved writers let it. Estelle couldn't be sure that her silence around the subject was helping or hurting her. Some readers had begged her to come forward with a statement, and some others assumed that her silence meant that she really had done something wrong.

Estelle was up to her ears in worry. Most of all, she was frightened this would implode her career. Who would purchase future books from a known plagiariser? She certainly wouldn't.

* * *

Charlie, Shawna, Sheila, and her new husband, Jonathon, invited Estelle and Roland out to dinner that night. Estelle tried to distract herself from everything in the bathroom, throwing herself into a makeup tutorial video Rachelle had shown her. When she pulled back from the mirror, she found that the smoky-eye she'd tried to give herself made her look like a gothic clown. She washed her face clean and patted it dry with her towel as, downstairs, Roland called to ask if she was nearly ready. Estelle then hurried through her normal makeup routine and fluffed her hair. During her seventy years on earth, she'd tried out nearly every beauty regime, every cat-eye, and every cleanser.

It occurred to her, as she swept from the bathroom, that both she and Margorie were the same age— seventy years old, locked together in a ridiculous internet feud. Wasn't that kind of thing reserved for pop singers in their twenties? Then again, there were many days in which Margorie felt just as young and naive as she had fifty years ago. Age was just a number— and this felt truer every year.

Charlie, Shawna, Sheila, and Jonathon were already at the table when Estelle and Roland arrived. Estelle swallowed Sheila in a hug, drawing herself back into the memories of Sheila's recent wedding. Sheila had been a stunning bride, and Jonathon's eyes had glistened with tears as he'd said his vows. Estelle and Roland had danced the night away, holding one another as the last slow song petered out and everyone returned to their hotel rooms. They'd outlasted several twenty-somethings, opening themselves up to whatever happened next.

"How's married life?" Roland asked as they adjusted around the table. "Answer very carefully, Jonathon." He winked.

Jonathon laughed nervously. "We were just talking about it today. It feels very special?" He glanced at Sheila as though he was frightened of using the wrong word.

"You must remember your first few months after your wedding," Sheila said, glancing between Estelle and Roland.

"You mean to tell me I've been married to this woman? For nearly fifty years?" Roland shook his head, feigning shock.

Sheila chuckled. "Did you forget?"

"I just don't know how I got so lucky," Roland said. "I never would have made it this far without her. That's for sure."

"That's not true," Estelle reminded him. "Your grand-father was different than most of the boys our age. He used to help me around the house, you know? Cooking and cleaning and mending things. Most of my girlfriends' husbands went to work, came home, and watched television, expecting them to care for the house and raise their children. But my Roland never did that."

"I paid her to brag about me tonight," Roland quipped.

Estelle squeezed Roland's thigh under the table. His silliness had taken her out of herself for a moment, and her smile felt natural, easy.

For dinner, Estelle ordered a tortellini dish, while Roland went with pork chops. Charlie suggested a red wine from the Aix-en-Provence region of France, and they agreed to try it out. After the waiter poured them each a glass, Charlie raised his to toast marriage. "Welcome to the fold, Sheila and Jonathon," he said. "May you have many happy years ahead of you."

As they ate, they discussed everything— island gossip, movies they'd watched, Chuck's care at the nursing home in Martha's Vineyard, and Estelle's time in New York, save for the allegations. Again, Shawna brought up the very strange story of Lisa, who'd once been engaged to Meghan's husband, Hugo, before disappearing without a trace twenty-five years ago. Recently, Lisa returned to the island to mend things with her family. She'd also come by Meghan and Hugo's place to apologize to Hugo to his face, which was a feat that required more bravery than Estelle could fully comprehend.

"Meghan said she could hardly sleep before Lisa came over," Shawna said. "Just like Hugo and Lisa, all of us here at the table were high school sweethearts. Somehow, it worked out for us." Shawna eyed Charlie nervously before adding, "I tried to imagine what it would be like not to see Charlie for twenty-five years and then suddenly have him there in front of me, meeting my husband."

"You tried to imagine that?" Charlie feigned shock.

"I just wanted to empathize with Hugo's situation." Shawna rolled her eyes. "It must have been very difficult."

"I think it's made Meghan and Hugo stronger," Roland said. "I talked to her on the phone the other day, and she said it's forced them to be really and truly honest for the first time in their lives."

"She was the love of Hugo's life," Sheila offered. "Lisa was just someone who didn't work out."

Shawna turned and gave Charlie a pointed look. "What else are you hiding, Charlie Coleman?"

"I should ask you the same thing, Shawna Coleman."

Everyone at the table laughed uproariously, and Estelle glanced at Roland, her heart filled with love. Of course, as a writer, she knew there were oceans of Roland's soul she would never know; that they were as close as two people could be, which was very intimate and very solitary at the same time. But it was impossible to poke through his psyche and point out everything she'd never known. Rather, being married to him had been a bit like watching the sun rise slowly over the ocean, its pinks and oranges and yellows flickering across the dark waters. She could only see what the sun reflected on the ocean, but under the surface of the water were depths she could never name. She knew she was the same; that, although she'd given him her heart, he would never know all of her. That might have terrified some, but to Estelle, that was endlessly romantic. It meant you were constantly learning.

Chapter Seven

1971

In early July, Estelle got a job at a restaurant to meet the demands of thousands upon thousands of tourists, who streamed off hourly ferries, set to explore the island, swim in the crisp waters of the Nantucket Sound, and eat to their hearts' content. The boss of the restaurant, a greasy man named Valentino, told Estelle she could put herself on the schedule whenever it suited her, and so Estelle worked around her mother's needs and appointments, never bothering to consider her own sleep requirements or mental health. Frequently, to get the smell of fried fish and French fries out of her hair, she went straight from work to the ocean and burst into the waves. Under the surface, she closed her eyes and screamed a sound nobody would ever hear.

Estelle saw Roland as much as she could, which was infrequently. Roland still operated under the belief that as soon as September rolled around, Estelle and Roland would be in their apartment in Amherst, building their new life. Estelle allowed him to talk about it openly if only to distract herself from her broken heart. He asked her questions about what towels they should buy, how many plates they needed, and whether or not they should buy a new vacuum cleaner or opt for the used one at the Coleman House. Every conversation sizzled with expectation for what came next, and Roland covered Estelle with kisses and promises for their next chapter. "As soon as your mother gets well again, we'll start over."

Roland had, of course, caught on that Estelle's father had left them. He'd noted the lack of cigarettes in the ashtray and the absence of Matt's truck in the driveway. "We haven't heard from him," Estelle explained with a shrug. "It's like he never existed at all."

Roland couldn't comprehend this. Although Meghan and Oriana had already been born on Martha's Vineyard, it would still be years before Roland learned of his own father's second family on Martha's Vineyard. In his mind, fathers kept their word to their wives and their children; they didn't abandon them, especially during Carrie's time of tremendous need. Roland's speeches about this subject made Estelle love him even harder. This would only make his leaving that much worse.

Sometimes, when Estelle couldn't sleep, she stood in front of the mirror in the hallway and practiced breaking up with Roland. "You deserve so much more than this," she rasped to the mirror. "You have a big future out there waiting for you. I don't want to hold you back." Every time she practiced, she slumped back into her bed and curled into a ball, waiting for the morning light to drown her bedsheets and force her into the non-stop routine of yet another day. At eighteen, she felt seventy or seventy-five years old. Her memories of being a carefree valedictorian seemed to belong to somebody else.

Estelle pushed the breakup as long as she could. By mid-August, their love had intensified, which only made the impending breakup feel that much worse. Roland spent the night at Estelle's place once or twice a week, sneaking out of the Coleman House after his parents went to sleep and waking up before dawn to hurry back home. Sometimes when he was over, he cleaned the kitchen or the bathroom or massaged Estelle's shoulders, anything to relieve her burdens.

But ten days before Roland was set to move to Amherst, Carrie's doctor imparted news that solidified Estelle's decision. Carrie wasn't getting better; they needed to do another round of treatment.

Carrie and Estelle sat in stunned silence in the front of Carrie's vehicle, Estelle in the driver's seat and Carrie in the passenger. She'd lost all of her hair, and she wore a straw sunhat that cast shadows across her face.

"I'm not doing another round of treatment," Carrie said in a low rasp.

Estelle cast her mother a look of anger.

"It's too much, honey," Carrie said, her eyes bloodshot with pain and fatigue. "I can't remember what it was like to feel normal. Maybe I never will again. Maybe that's something I have to accept."

Estelle took her mother's slender hand, which looked as small as a child's after her dramatic weight loss. "We've gotten through one round," Estelle whispered. "We can do another one."

Carrie's lower lip quivered. "You're not staying on this island, Estelle. You've worked too gosh-darn hard."

"So what? What does college matter?" Estelle alternated between anger and sorrow, dangerous emotions that left her reeling. "I want to be here with you, Mom. I want to help you through this. If you give up now, then what? What did the past few months mean?" She stuttered.

Carrie closed her eyes, and tears shot down her cheeks. "Even if I live, honey, I don't know if it matters. When I look in the mirror, I see something whittling down and dying."

"That's the illness," Estelle reminded her. "And the treatment. It's not you, Mom."

Carrie's breathing was ragged. Estelle knew she was thinking about her father.

"He didn't know how to handle it. He was a coward, and he didn't think things through," Estelle whispered. "He forgot that this isn't you. But you're going to get better, Mom. We have the best doctors in Nantucket."

The next thing Carrie said would echo in Estelle's mind for the rest of her days:

"I don't want to ruin your life."

Estelle gripped her mother's hand harder, on the brink of falling apart. "You gave me life, Momma. How could you ruin it?"

A few days later, after another treatment at the clinic, Estelle asked one of her friends to sit with her mother to make sure she got through the evening. "She might get sick," Estelle explained in a soft voice. "There's a pot already by the couch, and there's plenty of ginger ale in the fridge. Call Roland's place if anything gets really bad." She wrote Roland's house number on a pad of paper and left it on the counter, just in case.

Estelle hadn't been to the Coleman House for dinner in months. Walking up the driveway, she remembered the first time she'd ever been invited to meet his family. She'd been fifteen at the time, just a scrawny little thing, and when Chuck and Margaret had greeted her in their luxurious foyer, she'd felt like Cinderella at the ball. Now, as she rang the doorbell, she was struck with how bizarre it was that Roland had come from so much money while she'd come from so little. Their views of the world were probably completely different. Perhaps this was another reason to breakup. Probably, there would be numerous problems down the line— reasons to divorce.

Roland's mother, Margaret, opened the door and welcomed Estelle into a perfumed embrace. "You've been a stranger the past few months. Roland says you've been working yourself to death."

Estelle followed Margaret into the kitchen for a glass of iced tea and then to the back porch, where Roland, his brother, Grant, and his father, Chuck, talked politics. Roland and Grant were dressed like their father, with collared shirts that were better suited at the country club. Roland stood up to hug Estelle, and Grant popped up to give her a light punch on the arm. Because Estelle had always assumed she would marry Roland, she'd almost always considered Grant something like a brother. She hadn't considered how much she'd miss him, and the thought stung.

"Not long now till Amherst," Chuck said as she slipped onto the patio couch next to Roland. "How are you feeling?"

"Excited, I guess," Estelle lied.

"And you've already signed up for your classes?" Chuck asked.

"Yes. Several literature classes. One writing. Another history," Estelle said, although she hadn't even looked at the course manual since May.

"History of what?" Chuck asked. "They're all very specific. What did you say you're taking, Roland?"

"History of Medieval Europe," Roland announced.

"Right. Mine is History of..." Estelle's thoughts spun. "Architecture."

"Goodness! Architecture." Chuck's smile widened, showing too many of his teeth. "I never imagined you were keen on architecture. Tell me. Who's your favorite?"

Estelle's heart thudded with dread. Given her devastation, she couldn't recall a single architect's name and instead found her mind's eye filled with all the buildings she'd ever seen: her high school, her mother's shack, the Coleman House. Who had designed them? Did she care?

"She hasn't taken the class yet," Roland pointed out.

"Right. Ask me again in three months," Estelle said with a laugh.

Dinner lasted forever. Feeling in a nightmare, Estelle heard herself answer questions about their upcoming semester, about the apartment, and about her career plans as she choked down Margaret's roasted chicken. Margaret was a remarkable cook, and not eating everything she put in front of you was cause for alarm. Estelle didn't need any unwanted questions. When Margaret passed out lemon cream pie for dessert, Estelle choked that down, too.

After they cleared their plates, Estelle suggested to Roland that they walk along the beach. The night air was tinged with pink, and the Nantucket Sound sparkled and surged.

"We should," Roland said. "We'll miss the water when we go away."

At first, Estelle was petrified that Grant, Margaret,

and Chuck would want to go, too. But Grant soon disappeared in his bedroom, and Margaret insisted on getting a head-start on dishes. Chuck headed to his study, and soon after, the rancid smell of his cigar wafted from the top floor of the house.

Out on the sands, Roland was effervescent. He continued to discuss future plans as though everything he'd ever wanted would be handed to him on a silver platter. As a Coleman boy, that was expected. Estelle imagined him ten years from now, with four strapping sons and a gorgeous wife. Perhaps they'd return to Nantucket to raise them. Perhaps Estelle would have to see them around town, ducking behind telephone poles or abandoning her grocery cart if she stumbled into them at the store. Not everybody married their high school sweetheart, she tried to remind herself. But the thought alone felt like a knife.

"Roland." Estelle interrupted him and stopped short on the sand, stabbing her hands into the pockets of her miniskirt.

Roland turned to smile at her. "What's up?"

Estelle's chin quivered. She thought she might die on the spot. "Roland, I'm not going to college."

Roland's smile fell. "What are you talking about? Of course, you're going."

Estelle shook her head. "I can't."

Roland was speechless. He gaped at her as his dark curls fluttered around his ears and burst back with a violent wind.

"I have to stay here. My mother needs me. And there's nothing for me at college, you know? You're a Coleman. The entire world is out there, waiting for you." Estelle was grateful she wasn't crying. After weeks of weeping, it was as though she'd run out of tears. "And I can't hold you back. I refuse to."

Roland stitched his brows together. "But we have an apartment. We have plans. We've spent all summer talking about them."

Estelle raised her shoulders. "We both have plans. It just so happens that they're not the same plans anymore."

Roland reached for her hand, but Estelle dug it deeper into her pocket. She couldn't touch him. If she did, her entire resolve would crumble, and she would have to break up with him all over again in a few days.

"I've loved you so much, Roland," Estelle whispered, her voice wavering. "But we have to find a way to keep going without each other. I want you to go to Amherst and live as much as you can. I want you to fall in love with someone else. Someone who fits in with your Coleman world better. Someone who has more freedom."

"You fit," Roland blared. "You're all I want."

"You say that now," Estelle said. "But you'll change your mind in a few months. There are thousands of girls at the University of Massachusetts, Roland. There has to be one you like."

Estelle felt she was being reasonable, as though she were a scientist presenting her research to a team of doctors. After all, she'd spent all summer reminding herself this was the only way forward. But the way Roland looked at her now made her feel like an alien.

"I can't talk to you right now," Roland shot, his face losing its color. "I can't even look at you." He then turned on his heel and stomped back toward the Coleman House, a mansion at the top of the bluffs. As he went, Estelle stared at him, feeling as though she'd just been slapped. She wondered if that was the last conversation she would ever have with Roland – if, after four and a half years of kisses and laughter and long, soulful conversations, it would end like this: with Roland stomping away from her on the beach. She prayed this wasn't how he would remember her. She would certainly spend the next few hours deleting this scene from her mind.

Too embarrassed to go back inside where she wasn't wanted, Estelle slunk around the side of the house, slipped into her car, and sped back home. By the time she returned, her body had found a new source of tears, and the world was blurry with the devastation of what she'd done. She knew it was the right thing— but sometimes, the right thing broke your heart. And when she saw her mother that night, her breathing ragged as she curled up on her thin mattress, she told herself to be strong.

Chapter Eight

M argorie hardly recognized herself. She stood at the kitchen counter in a robe, her feet snuggled up in slippers, and scraped a pad of butter across an English muffin as soft snow swirled through the winter winds. Christmas music twinkled from her Bluetooth speaker, classics from the sixties and seventies, and Margorie caught herself humming as she brought a crispy half of English muffin to her lips. For the past three nights, she'd tossed and turned, her mind awash with thoughts of Daniel: what he looked like, how he laughed. She could hear his voice in her head, echoing. What had gotten into her?

Daniel had told her to come by the store "any time" to sign copies of her novels for his regulars. But Margorie struggled with whether or not to believe he really meant it. Perhaps he was just another lonely man at a restaurant. Perhaps he spoke to every other lonely woman when he was out, just to pass the time. Perhaps.

But then again, Margorie had spoken to him first.

Margorie took her mug of coffee to the study down the hall. This was a ritual, one she hoped would eventually spark a few words across the keyboard. But when she sat at her computer, surrounded by her heavy bookshelves and her photographs of friends from long-ago vacations, she was stumped. Writer's block was a perpetual weight on her chest, one that disallowed her to dig into the creative side of her mind and allow a story to flow freely from the tips of her fingers. Why had it been so easy before?

To distract herself, Margorie pulled up her social media to find that the #TeamMargorie and #TeamEstelle dispute had intensified. People weren't dropping it, and her sales had tripled in the previous week. Would this bring the boost of confidence she so needed?

Margorie showered and changed into a navy wool sweater and a pair of high-waisted jeans. After she styled her long, red locks, she touched up her face and smiled at her reflection, trying to imagine what Daniel saw when he looked at her. He was younger, yes, but not by much. They'd both been trampled by life in one way or another. They'd both come through on the other side.

Margorie drove to The White Whale Bookstore with her heart in her throat. Street parking in front was minimal, but she grabbed a spot at the last-minute and parallel parked perfectly. This was the only skill her father had ever passed down to her, a result of screaming at her until she performed it correctly. A shiver ran up her spine as she got out and strode toward the porch of the little Victorian home in which Daniel rented space for his bookstore. It looked like a fairytale.

A bell above the door jangled as Margorie entered the

warmth of the shop. Daniel was off in the corner with three women in their eighties, who gushed about a recent women's fiction series Daniel had recommended to them. As Marjorie closed the door behind her, Daniel spun to say hello, and his face was illuminated with surprise.

"Welcome to the shop!" he said. "I'll be with you in just a second."

"Take your time," Margorie assured him.

Beside Daniel, the three eighty-something women ogled them both, having sensed something within their tones— a flirtation, perhaps. Margorie forced herself to the opposite side of the bookstore, where she lifted books from their shelves nervously, hardly able to read their blurbs.

All of the women purchased books from Daniel and wished Margorie a Merry Christmas on their way out. One of them suggested hot cocoa; another said she had to leave for a hair appointment. The door rushed closed with another jangle, leaving Margorie and Daniel alone in the store. A blush crawled up the back of Marjorie's neck. She could feel Daniel's gaze upon her, then heard his footsteps.

"Fantasy?" Daniel asked.

"What?" Margorie jumped and realized she held a fantasy novel in her hand. A painting of a dragon wrapped around from the back to the front. How had she picked up a fantasy book without noticing? "Oh, yes. I know these kinds of books are really popular. I've never read them. Should I start?"

"If it's not your thing, it's not your thing," Daniel offered. "I don't mind a fantasy epic every now and again, but I know it's not for everyone."

Margorie's heartbeat felt out of rhythm. Every time

she allowed herself to look Daniel in the eye, she lost all track of her thoughts.

"This bookstore is gorgeous," she said. "I can't believe I've never come in here before."

"And I can't believe you came! I had lost hope."

He'd been waiting for her? Margorie's throat tightened.

"I know you're busy," Daniel hurried to add. "You're probably writing a few books right now. I'm just grateful you made the time."

Was he flirting with her? Or did he just really want her to sign copies of her books for his regulars? Margorie's instincts around dating were more than rusty.

Daniel led Margorie to the romance section, where he had four of her books on the shelf— including *A Christmas Dream*. A brief glance told Margorie that he didn't have any Estelle Coleman books on-hand. Did he know about the feud? Had he hidden them away so as not to upset her?

Daniel removed the books from the shelf and handed Margorie a pen. Nervously, she scrawled her name on the title pages of each.

"Did you practice that when your books started selling?" Daniel asked.

Margorie dropped her head back with laughter.

"I'm sorry," Daniel hurried to say. "That was rude of me."

"No! It wasn't rude. To tell you the truth, I wanted to be a writer so badly as a kid. I practiced my signature like crazy."

"As a kid? Wow." Daniel shook his head. "It's rare that people actually go after and achieve their dreams, you know?"

It had been a long time since Margorie had reminded herself of this: that she'd made a goal and actually reached it. Why had she allowed herself to forget?

"Listen," Daniel said as he slid the books back onto the shelf, along with a placard that said: SIGNED BOOKS. "An employee is coming to the store in about twenty minutes to take over. If you don't have plans, would you like to walk over to the Christmas Market with me?"

Margorie's heart thumped. "Christmas Market?" She hadn't heard anything about that.

Daniel's blush was tomato-red. "They decorated the area by the port like an old German village. There are little wooden houses selling hot wine, pizzas, and chocolate. My daughter and her husband went the other day, and they even tried hot beer!"

Margorie wrinkled her nose. "That sounds disgusting!"

"Doesn't it? But it made me curious." Daniel gave her a hopeful smile. "If you don't have time, don't worry about it. I'm just grateful for the signed books."

"It sounds wonderful," Margorie said before she could chicken out. "Let's go."

* * *

Daniel and Margorie walked side-by-side through the cruel blasts of Martha's Vineyard winds, headed toward the harbor. Overhead, Christmas lights were strewn from one side of the street to the other, and they twinkled on as they walked. It was only four, but already, the sky overhead was thick with dark clouds, and night would fall soon.

"Do you hear that?" Daniel asked, tilting his head as they rounded a corner.

Margorie perked her ears to hear the jangle of Christmas music. A few steps later, the pointed tops of the Germanic wooden stalls came into view, along with a cozy sea of people dressed in many layers of Christmas garb, their gloved hands around mugs of cocoa or mulled wine. As a rush of excitement swelled through Margorie's chest, she stalled, and Daniel glanced back at her curiously.

"Sorry," Margorie said, hurrying to align herself with him. "I felt like a little kid again. Just for a moment."

Daniel touched her back gently, his eyes illuminated. It was the first time he'd ever touched her on purpose like that, his fingertips inches away from her skin due to the thickness of her coat, scarf, and sweater. Even still, it felt like lightning.

Daniel and Margorie strolled through the Christmas Market. Daniel waved at several Oak Bluffs residents with a smile, and Margorie said, "You know everyone around here."

"I really don't," Daniel assured her. "I was gone for too long. Because I spent so many decades in California, they don't fully recognize me as an islander anymore."

"They think California changed you?"

Daniel laughed. "I don't know. What do you think?"

Margorie's heart thumped. All she saw when she looked at Daniel was a handsome and intellectual man who, for whatever reason, had decided to spend his afternoon with her.

"I think people get stuck on labeling each other," Margorie said. "We want everyone to fit into molds and boxes, like me. I'm a romance writer who lost her husband. I'm a cliché, right?"

Daniel furrowed his brow. "You're not a cliché in the slightest."

"That's what I mean," Margorie assured him. "Nobody is a cliché. Everyone is a walking, talking contradiction, and I wish more people gave each other space for that."

"Well said." Daniel touched her shoulder this time, and his eyes glistened. "Sometimes I feel like a cliché, too. I'm a divorcé who owns a bookstore. I belong in a Meg Ryan movie."

Margorie's lips quivered into a smile. "Do you think Tom Hanks would play you?"

"No way," Daniel said. "Tom Hanks is way too dashing for me. Maybe Steve Buscemi?"

Margorie cackled into her hand. Daniel looked as though he'd just won the lottery, as though making her laugh was his greatest achievement.

"Do you want a mug of mulled wine?" Daniel suggested. "I need to warm up."

Margorie and Daniel waited in line for seven minutes, shivering as they drew closer to the front. Once there, a man in a Santa hat poured them two mugs and passed them over. Daniel paid without glancing Margorie's way — more proof this was a date.

Daniel clinked his mug with hers and said, "To you, Margorie. And to living outside the box."

Now that Margorie had revealed she was a widow and Daniel had called himself a "divorcé," the air had shifted, and there was a new intimacy between them. Margorie couldn't believe she'd revealed that so easily. It wasn't like her to show her cards.

Daniel explained more about his reasons for returning to the Vineyard after a lifetime in California. "When my mother's doctor called about her dementia diagnosis, I explained the situation to my wife at the time. We were on the rocks, and things weren't looking good. I think we both believed Martha's Vineyard was our last shot at a life together. Obviously, it didn't work." Daniel raised his shoulders.

"She went back to California?"

Daniel nodded. "But my daughter, her husband, and her son live out here with me right now. Actually, we have a pretty full house now that my sister came home." He sipped his wine and gazed out across the frothing water just beyond the harbor railing. "My sister, Lisa, disappeared about twenty-five years ago. We always had a difficult relationship, so when people were fighting to figure out what happened to her, I was terrified for her to return. But when she did, she revealed herself to be a completely different sort of person. One filled with compassion."

This triggered a memory. "Wait a minute. This isn't related to the 'Find Lisa' photographs and pamphlets that were all over the island a few weeks ago?"

"The very same."

Margorie's eyes widened. For a little while, the photograph of the twenty-five-year-old blonde woman had peered out from every shop window and every bulletin board. Those looking for her had put upwards of fifteen pamphlets in Margorie's mailbox, consistently reminding Margorie of this Vineyard ghost.

The missing signs had ignited something in Margorie, and she'd even considered writing a book about the young woman. She'd jotted down a few notes to herself about a fictional Lisa who'd gone into hiding after heartbreak.

Funnily enough, Daniel explained that was part of the reason Lisa had left the Vineyard in the first place.

"You were going to write a book about her?" Daniel asked, surprised.

"No! Not really. I was just so curious about her," Margorie explained. "I'd never known anyone to go missing before. I found myself making up stories about what could have happened. But it sounds like the very best version of this story already played out."

"I can't tell you how relieved I am that she's safe," Daniel agreed. "Maybe you can meet her sometime. She's sharp as a tack and reads almost as voraciously as we do."

"I'd like that."

In real life, Margorie had very few friends and even fewer family members. But as she and Daniel walked around the market, snacking on cheese bread and tantalizing chocolate fudge, Margorie allowed herself to fall into the story of Daniel. Perhaps this was a new chapter, one that would allow her to dismiss the sorrows of the previous few years.

When Daniel tugged her glove from her hand and swept his fingers through hers, he asked, "Is this all right?" Margorie's throat was too tight to answer. All she could do was nod.

Margorie fell through the daydream of the early evening and floated back home to cozy up by the fire and stare into space. She was reminded of the early days of meeting Tom when she'd felt so out of her mind with love that she'd forgotten appointments and missed deadlines. This late in the game, it felt impossible she was allowed to feel like this. Maybe there was something wrong with her brain.

Just as she got up to pour herself a fresh mug of tea,

Margorie's phone pinged. It was an article from a magazine called *The Literary Romantic*, and it was titled: "Is Estelle Coleman a Con-Artist?" Immediately, Margorie returned to her nest on the couch and dropped herself into the article.

Although the article presented no new facts, it laid out the details of Margorie and Estelle's feud, showing social media postings of their fans and noting the tremendous rise in sales for both parties. The article also didn't take a side. Maybe that was too much to hope for. Still, the title alone referred to Estelle Coleman as a con-artist, which had to help Margorie's case.

Margorie had genuinely tried to like Estelle Coleman. They'd met one another at several romance writer conventions and had even shared a glass of wine or two. Estelle had been shivery with nerves, proof of her greenness in the industry, and she'd looked at Margorie as though Margorie knew a secret about writing that she refused to share. In her own ears, Margorie had sounded upbeat and enlightened during these conversations, but internally, she'd wondered if Estelle was messing with her. Didn't Estelle know who Margorie was? Didn't she remember?

Chapter Nine

1971

On the day Roland was set to leave for Amherst, Estelle worked a ten-hour shift at the restaurant. She burst from the kitchen and back again, her arms laden with very heavy trays of fish filets, French fries, tartar sauce, and steak, her feet and legs screaming with each impact on the tiled floor. It was late summer, and tourists were especially needy, their faces and shoulders red with sunburn, their children wailing with hunger and thirst. Estelle did her best not to look at the clock. Each time she forgot, she thought to herself: *"Roland's an hour away,"* or *"Roland's probably in the apartment by now,"* or *"Roland's probably eating dinner. Maybe at that pizza place."* Roland had begun his new life without her, just as she'd requested. And she was having trouble not resenting herself for digging this hole and lying in it.

Estelle got off work at ten-thirty and went for a long walk along the harbor. Around her, the same grumpy tourists from the restaurant were now euphoric, drinking beers or eating ice cream cones. Their laughter echoed across the black Nantucket Sound. Estelle studied their faces as her stomach tightened. Roland wasn't on the island. Roland wasn't off at his parents' place, waiting for her to get off work so they could meet. Roland was away. And there was no telling if she would ever see him again.

Sick with sorrow, Estelle hurried back into the restaurant to throw up. Her knees rattled together, and tears spilled from her eyes. When she got out of the bathroom, her boss accused her of drinking too much, but she told him she hadn't had a drop. At that moment, she hated him so much that she wanted to quit— but she knew she couldn't. She still needed as second job.

Carrie's second round of treatment didn't seem to be going any better than the first. She was frequently too ill to stand or walk and almost never wanted to eat. Worry hung over their house like a thick cloud. Estelle tip-toed around, not wanting to wake her. When she needed to wake her up for an appointment or a round of treatment, she did so as gently as she could.

During that first week that Roland was gone, Estelle slept fitfully and had many nightmares. In them, Roland was in Amherst, already falling in love with someone else. He was studying to be an astrophysicist; he was receiving award after award; his very attractive girlfriend was already pregnant. In one dream, he announced, "Estelle was my childhood love. Isn't that cute?" Bizarrely, Estelle never saw herself in these dreams. Maybe this was because her life was officially over anyway. Even her psyche knew that.

One week after Roland moved to Amherst, Estelle went to the library before work. With soft light cascading through the windows and down the aisles, it felt like a sacred place, almost church-like. She stood between aisles of fiction and touched the spines of old books, willing herself to choose a fictional world to fall into. It would be a perfect escape.

"Estelle?" A whisper rasped from the other side of the aisle.

Estelle nearly jumped out of her skin. Her first thought was that it was a library ghost haunting her.

Instead, it was Roland's Aunt Jessabelle, who worked at the library. Carrying a stack of books, she floated down the aisle toward Estelle, wearing a confident and beautiful smile. At Coleman family functions, Estelle had always been drawn to Jessabelle, to her literary nature and her insistence on living by her own rules. Perhaps this was because Jessabelle wasn't a Coleman at all— she was Margaret's sister.

"There she is," Jessabelle said. "The writer."

Estelle's cheeks burned with embarrassment. It felt like years ago that she'd told Jessabelle her dream of becoming a writer one day. That was about as likely as pigs flying.

"I'm just a reader these days," Estelle admitted. "Although I haven't had much time this summer."

A wrinkle of worry formed between Jessabelle's eyebrows. She placed the stack of books on a cart beside her and crossed her arms. Estelle prayed she wouldn't bring up Roland. She could barely stand to hear his name.

"I saw you working at that restaurant by the harbor," Jessabelle said instead. "I've heard terrible things about the boss."

Estelle wrinkled her nose. "Valentino's not my favorite person in the world. But I need the work."

Jessabelle raised her shoulders. "I'm looking to hire someone here at the library. With autumn and winter coming, more people borrow books. And, of course, most of those people turn their books in late, which adds another layer of work for us librarians. We have to chase them down and make them pay their dues."

"Sounds dangerous," Estelle joked.

Jessabelle laughed, and Estelle realized this was the first time she'd cracked a joke in months. It made her feel a part of the world in a very small way.

"I'd love to have you around, Estelle," Jessabelle said. "You were valedictorian of your class. Having that intellect around the library is never a bad thing. Plus, you can borrow whatever books you want."

Estelle was tempted. Behind Jessabelle was a clock that ticked ever more toward her scheduled shift at the restaurant, and her stomach tightened with dread.

"I need a second job," Estelle admitted, hating how pathetic she sounded.

Jessabelle nodded. "We can work around your restaurant schedule. No problem at all. When are you going next?"

"In about five minutes."

"Write down your week's schedule for me," Jessabelle instructed. "Bring it by tomorrow morning, and I'll assign you some shifts."

Estelle's heart thumped. She wanted to gush to Jessabelle about the library; she wanted to tell her that it was the only place she'd felt safe in since the day of her high school graduation. But saying such things aloud to a person as emotionally tuned-in as Jessabelle was unnecessary. Jessabelle understood.

* * *

Jessabelle assigned Estelle twenty hours of work at the library alongside Estelle's thirty-five hours at the restaurant, promising that her hours could go up as soon as the restaurant hours went down. Never once did Jessabelle ask Estelle about her mother's treatments or Roland's departure, which made the library feel outside of time. Those terrible things hadn't actually happened there. Sometimes, as Estelle shelved books or wrote letters asking where missing books were, she pretended that Roland was at the beach, waiting for her, that her father and mother were out for a walk and planned to come see her at the library. It was this capacity for daydreaming that would have made her a good novelist; she knew that. But she also had no idea how to start.

Besides, now that she had no plans to go to university, she didn't have any real hope for her future. Maybe she could continue on at the library for a long time and eventually take over Jessabelle's post. There were worse things.

After two weeks at the library, Estelle had found an easy flow. She knew the regulars, could shelve books with her eyes closed, and even kept snacks in the refrigerator. It was September, and the air had shifted outside, chasing tourists back to wherever they'd come from. Roland felt further away than ever.

"I have to run," Estelle told Jessabelle as she finished shelving a cart of books. Her mother's treatment was later that afternoon, and she wanted to clean the kitchen before they left.

"Your shift was over ten minutes ago!" Jessabelle pointed at the clock.

"I know." Estelle laughed. "But once I got started on this cart, I didn't want to abandon it."

Jessabelle clucked her tongue, crossed her arms, and leaned against a towering bookshelf. She looked captivated by Estelle. Estelle faltered as she slid a final book onto the shelf.

"I have something for you," Jessabelle told her.

"You didn't have to do that."

"You don't even know what it is yet." Jessabelle beckoned for Estelle to follow her down the aisle and toward the mahogany front desk. There, she whirled around, ducked to search through a shelf, and retrieved a wrapped gift. It was obviously a book.

"I wonder what it is," Estelle joked as Jessabelle pressed it across the counter.

"Open it," Jessabelle urged her.

Estelle tore at the wrapping paper gently to reveal its title: *How to Write a Novel.* Something cold and hard dropped into her stomach, and she couldn't force a smile.

"Wow," she said, her tone dark. "Thank you."

Jessabelle touched Estelle's wrist. "I have a copy of my own. I love it. It gives you little writing exercises to do and helps you plot your first novel. I'm not very far on mine yet. I might never finish it! But I have a hunch about you. I know you have a lot of stories to tell."

Estelle swallowed the lump in her throat and heard herself thank Jessabelle again. She was the only person Estelle could count on right now. She couldn't unleash her anger upon her, even if she felt it boiling up in her veins. How on earth could she write a novel right now? Where would she find the time? And didn't Jessabelle know that her heart was just as broken as her mind right now?

"Thank you," Estelle said again, raising the corners of her lips. "I can't wait to get started."

Back at home, Estelle threw the book as hard as she could under her bed, and it snapped against the wall. She felt childish. In the kitchen, she scrubbed the countertops and the stove, trying and failing not to picture Roland in Amherst, perhaps sharing pizza with a gorgeous young woman. "Both of our families had money," she imagined Roland saying. "We understood each other immediately."

But no. Her version of Roland would never say that. The version of Roland, who now lived in her head was monstrous. How could she get rid of him?

Estelle drove her mother to the treatment clinic and sat in the waiting room reading a novel she'd taken from the library. She was glad she'd gotten back into reading. All the magazines in the clinic waiting room were the same as they'd been in June. When her mother returned from the back room, she was pale as milk and very soft-spoken. Estelle pushed her wheelchair out to the car and helped her into the passenger seat, where she laid back against the headrest, her breathing ragged.

And then, she said something that would stick with Estelle for the rest of her life.

"You've been so good to me," Carrie rasped. "I never deserved it."

"I love you, Mom," Estelle said in only a whisper. She realized she hadn't said it in so long— these words that had once been so easy for her. She'd said them continually to her mother and Roland. They'd been a kind of song.

Estelle got her mother to bed that night and stayed up late, her head pounding with a headache she couldn't shake. Outside, a violent storm ripped across the island, and rain pelted against the windowpanes. She thought again of Jessabelle, all alone after her husband had left her for another woman. The rumor was that Jessabelle couldn't get pregnant; her ex had wanted children. Yet there wasn't a trace of that sorrow in Jessabelle's eyes. How had she gotten rid of it? Or had she just learned to carry it gracefully?

Chapter Ten

Present Day

The "Is Estelle Coleman a Con-Artist" article sent shockwaves through the literary community. Estelle watched it play out across social media as though it were a volcanic blast. There was nothing to be done about it. The feud had taken on new heights.

Although Estelle adored her family, she hated sounding like a broken record. She watched herself perform a different version of herself at Christmas, buying even more decorations for the tree and around the house, playing Christmas music at all hours, and going shopping for her children and grandchildren like a mad woman. Her closets were stuffed to the gills with wrapping paper, little trinkets, cashmere sweaters, books and notebooks, paintings, and the like. Roland had begun to call her the Christmas Monster.

On the morning of December 13th, Estelle woke up

to an email that changed her life. It was from her agent, Christie, and it said, simply, "Call me."

Estelle made a pot of coffee and locked herself in her office. There, she placed her phone against her ear and listened as it blared out. Christie answered on the third ring.

"Hi." Christie sounded strained. "I have some bad news."

"Okay. Hit me." Estelle steeled herself, trying to remind herself that she'd been through horrific times in her life. She'd gotten through all of them. This was hardly a blip.

"The publishing house has rescinded their offer on the series," Christie said.

Estelle was woozy, and she collapsed on the chair behind her. Just months ago, a top-rated romance publishing house had asked her to write a six-book romance series set on Nantucket Island. The advance they'd pitched had been spectacular, and they'd been in the midst of setting the deal in stone when this Margorie Tomlinson feud had begun.

"I did my best to explain that you didn't steal a thing from that woman," Christie went on. "That she's using you for book sales. But honestly, it doesn't seem to matter whether you did or didn't do it."

"My name is mud," Estelle affirmed, trying to laugh. "I can't believe it."

"Just keep writing," Christie assured her. "This will all blow over eventually, and the publishing house will be kicking themselves for missing this opportunity with you."

But Estelle wasn't so sure. After they hung up, she sat at

the window, her coffee forgotten, and tried to make peace with the idea that her writing career was over. It wasn't so bad, was it? After all, she'd had decent success over the years; she'd had a book launch in Manhattan; she'd made friends with numerous readers who appreciated her view of the world. That was more than most writers were allowed.

Around noon, Estelle left her office to find Roland at the kitchen counter, making a sandwich. She wrapped her arms around his stomach and pressed her face into the wool of his sweater. His body vibrated as he spoke about what he'd read in the newspaper, about the crossword clue he couldn't get, and about the basketball game he planned to watch with Charlie that evening. Estelle remembered a time when she'd thought Roland was a part of her past, someone better-off forgotten. She reminded herself to thank her lucky stars that he was there, in her kitchen, wrapped in her arms. They'd enjoyed decades of marriage together.

When Estelle returned to her office with a bowl of oatmeal with fruit, she dialed a fellow romance novelist named Lucinda. They'd been friends for nearly twenty years at this point, having met in a Nantucket writing group way back in the day. That was before Lucinda had moved to Maine and published her top-selling romance series— one that had a bit more spice than Estelle used in her books. It had sold like hotcakes.

Lucinda answered on the second ring, her tone overly-bright, as though she knew already why Estelle called.

"Hello, darling! It's so good to hear from you."

Estelle crossed her legs and turned her rolly chair toward the window. "Lucinda. How are you?"

"I'm doing just fine. Freezing cold here in Maine, but that's to be expected."

"You Maine folks are heartier than we are down here," Estelle agreed.

The two of them exchanged small-talk for a few minutes, easing toward the topic at-hand. Finally, Estelle broached it.

"Did you happen to see what's been going on with Margorie Tomlinson?"

Lucinda's tone darkened. "It's been a mess, hasn't it?"

"Completely." Estelle furrowed her brow. For some reason, she'd expected Lucinda to be immediately on her side, jumping at the chance to tell Estelle just how in the wrong Margorie was. "I haven't known what to do with myself. And my most recent book deal just fell through this morning."

"Oh, goodness. I just hate that."

Estelle grimaced and stood to her feet to pace through the study. She hated how much she wanted to convince Lucinda of her innocence right now. "You know," she began, "I wrote *A Bright Christmas* based on my own experiences?"

"Is that so?" Lucinda sounded doubtful.

"Yes," Estelle stuttered. "It's from a time when I was eighteen. My mother was very sick, and I..."

"You don't have to explain yourself to me," Lucinda assured her. Her tone shimmered with confusion.

"I just can't understand why Margorie would do this. I always thought we were friendly, at the very least," Estelle said. "Can you think of a way I can prove that this was my story from the beginning?"

Lucinda was quiet. Somewhere on the other line was the soft murmur of a television. Estelle wondered if

Lucinda was only giving her half of her attention. She now fully regretted calling Lucinda at all. This wasn't the comfort she'd yearned for.

"Did you ever meet Margorie?" Estelle asked.

"I did," Lucinda said. "She's such a beauty, isn't she? That red hair!"

Estelle rolled her eyes. "Yes. She is. But did she seem, I don't know, dishonest to you?"

"Not especially," Lucinda said. "Although you know how this business can be. Cut-throat."

"I'm embarrassed to say that I never thought of it that way," Estelle said softly. "I loved reading everyone's work. I felt like there was enough space for all of us."

"Oh, honey. No business is like that."

Lucinda sounded judgmental. Was it better for Lucinda to think Estelle was naive rather than guilty?

"I just can't decide if I should reach out to her," Estelle offered. "I want to explain myself, but I don't want to make things worse." She bit her lower lip before adding, "You don't happen to know where she lives, do you?"

"Margorie? No. She went off the grid several years ago," Lucinda said. "I looked through her social media just the other day, and there are no recent photographs. Nothing since her husband's death five years ago."

Estelle's heart seized. "Oh. Oh, no."

News of Margorie's husband's death shot through her.

"It was really sudden," Lucinda went on. "After that, I heard Margorie left their little town in upstate New York. I can only assume it was too painful to stay."

Estelle filled her lungs, feeling woozy. "I can't even imagine."

"A romance writer who loses her husband! It's just terrible," Lucinda agreed. "I don't blame her for not writing another book."

Estelle couldn't think of anything else to say. Drawing attention back to losing her contract seemed tactless. Eventually, she asked Lucinda about her current book project, her grandchildren, and her love of ice fishing, grateful for the normalcy in her tone. She then got off the phone and stared out the window, lost in thought.

It was tragic that Margorie had lost her husband. But Estelle had worked tirelessly to build her career. She hated watching her career slip through the cracks, all because of Margorie's vendetta against her. Where had it come from? Why was it happening? And was everyone, like Lucinda, beginning to believe Margorie was correct?

Chapter Eleven

1971

Margorie Ratner was a freshman at the University of Massachusetts in Amherst. A scrawny thing with long, wild red hair, she was jittery and nervous around most classmates, frequently keeping to herself and reading at the library over the weekend rather than making friends. She was fifty miles from her family's home, fifty miles from her father's vitriol and her mother's depression. It never felt like enough space between them. She never really felt free.

Margorie lived on campus in a dorm room with a roommate who hated her. The roommate's name was Sylvia, and she was athletic and beautiful, with miniskirts that showed off her long, tan legs and a different boyfriend every week. Sometimes, Margorie eavesdropped on Sylvia's conversations with these boys, studying what she said and how she said it. Where had Sylvia learned to be so mysterious? So feminine?

Margorie couldn't imagine speaking to men like that. It seemed no secret to the world that she'd never been kissed. Romance was something that happened to other people, not her.

Perhaps because she'd never been in love, Margorie was obsessed with writing about it. She filled notebooks with fantasy stories about men and women who were "made for each other," who met each other in adorable seaside towns or in the middle of New York City bookstores. She often practiced her signature in these notebooks, dreaming about the future, when, she hoped, she would fall in love and become a famous writer, all in one fell swoop. By then, she wouldn't be an awkward, quiet, moody girl of eighteen. She'd be someone else. Someone better.

Margorie's favorite class was English Literature from the 1800s, where they read everything from Jane Austen to George Eliot to H.G. Wells. Like any good romance-lover, Margorie adored Jane Austen and often reread chapters of her books, captivated by the way Austen drew her characters. Despite nearly two hundred years between them, Margorie saw her shyness and her fear in characters like Jane and Mary, yet craved the extraversion of Elizabeth or Kitty.

Margorie sat toward the back of every classroom, and English Literature was no different. She liked to sit and listen to the students discussing the text around her, raising their hands easily to divulge their thoughts to the professor. All throughout September and into October, Margorie sat in stunned silence, gripping each of the books, wondering if she would ever have the bravery to raise her hand and add her two cents. It wasn't that she didn't have numerous thoughts about these books— and in fact, her essays always came back with good grades. But hearing her voice aloud petrified her.

In mid-October, they discussed *Jane Eyre* by Charlotte Brontë. Prior to the classroom talk, Margorie sat at her desk and wrote notes to herself about what she'd thought about the first fifty pages. A stream of students entered the classroom and peppered themselves over the available desks, chatting about what had happened that weekend and what parties they'd attended. One of them was Roland Coleman, a six-foot-three statue of a man with wild black curls and eyes that seemed to pierce through you. Margorie couldn't help but glance up as he approached his usual desk, which was kitty-corner to Margorie's. If she was honest with herself, when Margorie wrote little romantic stories in her journals, Roland was almost always the hero. Her reasons for this went far beyond his looks. Number one: he was probably the most brilliant student in the class. Unlike most of the other boys, he hadn't rebuked Jane Austen and had even gushed over Austen's beautiful sentences. Number two: he didn't act as though Margorie was an invisible ghost who wasn't worthy of his attention.

Now, Roland removed *Jane Eyre* from his backpack, ruffled his curls, and glanced back at Margorie, who was careful to avert her eyes. "Hey! Margorie."

"What's up?" Margorie's voice was higher pitched than she'd planned for, probably proof of her nerves.

Roland's eyes were slits. "What did you think about that scene on page eighteen? I wanted to talk about it today in class, but I feel like I approached it incorrectly."

Margorie's heart thumped as she thumbed through her book. Why was he asking her for help?

"I know you have a mastery of these things," Roland

explained to Margorie. "I had a chat with Professor Gregor the other day, and he said you have the top grades on essays in the class."

Margorie's cheeks were flushed. She'd made her way to page eighteen, but she couldn't draw her eyes away from Roland's. He was looking at her the way she'd always dreamt he would: as though she were the only person in the world he cared about.

"I thought, um," Margorie began, just as Professor Gregor burst through the door and placed his briefcase on the desk. The classroom quieted, but Professor Gregor noted Margorie's open mouth and open book, gestured toward her, and said, "Margorie! Do you have something you'd like to say about the text?"

A shiver raced up and down Margorie's spine. Roland gave her a firm nod of recognition, proof he believed in her. And then, overcome with a sense of bravery and confidence Margorie had never felt before, she said, "I thought Charlotte Brontë struggled in this book."

The classroom quieted and gaped at Margorie. It wasn't customary to insult the long-dead writer they discussed.

"Please. Explain," Professor Gregor urged.

Margorie's cheeks were painfully warm. "It feels like Brontë herself struggled with the concept of reason versus passion," she went on, fumbling her words.

Professor Gregor crossed his arms over his chest and set his jaw. "Reason versus passion," he repeated.

Margorie was suddenly terrified she'd said something wrong. All the other students exchanged glances as though on the verge of insinuating Margorie was an idiot.

"Jane has this incredible passion throughout the text," Margorie went on. "And she dips into that passion to drive herself forward. But as time goes on, she has to reel it in. If she doesn't, her passion for life is bound to destroy her."

Professor Gregor dropped his chin toward his chest. Still, nobody spoke. Margorie had begun to suspect this was all a terrible dream.

And then, Professor Gregor said, "Did everyone hear what Margorie just explained to us?"

The other students glanced at Margorie confusedly and nodded.

Professor Gregor pointed in her general direction. "That is a well-thought-out argument. That is the sort of thing to build an entire thesis upon. If any of you need help getting started on your papers for *Jane Eyre*, run your ideas past Margorie. She has a good handle on things."

As Professor Gregor moved on to another student, who stuttered through the concept of *Jane Eyre*'s characterization, Roland turned back to wink at Margorie. Margorie had never been winked at before, and it nearly startled her out of her seat. She smiled back and floated through the rest of the afternoon until she collapsed on her dorm bed to stare at the ceiling and daydream. Sylvia's newest boyfriend was a jock who spoke slower than anyone Margorie had ever heard. He couldn't hold a candle to Roland.

Over the next week or two, Margorie pushed herself to be braver in class. She raised her hand during the discussion, contradicted things other students said, and even admitted to Professor Gregor she didn't side with his argument on a literary matter. Sometimes after class, Roland paused as he gathered his things and sidled up next to her, and they walked through the first hallway together, continuing their discussion about Jane Eyre.

Sometimes, he lingered for so long in the hallway with her, adjusting the straps of his backpack nervously, that they were both nearly late for their next class.

"What do you have after this?" Roland asked after two weeks of this arrangement.

"French. And you?"

"German!" Roland laughed. "Why don't we walk together? It's the same building."

It was insane to them both that they'd always separated and walked in different directions to the same location. Their laughter echoed through the hallway as they escaped the ornate stone building and swept across campus. As they went, they passed other boys and girls, men and women, some of whom held hands. Margorie eyed Roland's own hand, shifting gently by his side as they walked toward the foreign language department. Would she ever get the opportunity to hold it? Would she ever dare to tell him how she felt?

By the time November rolled around, Margorie and Roland had taken to eating dinner together after their foreign language classes on Tuesdays and Thursdays. Usually, the meal in the dining hall was chicken or pizza, something simple and greasy, and they grabbed a table near the window of the large dining hall and chatted about anything that came to their minds. Roland was now officially Margorie's "friend," her only one on campus, and she felt at-ease around him in ways she hadn't since her most-recent best friend, Kathy, who'd moved away from Margorie's hometown at age twelve.

"It was like having a target on my back all the time," Roland explained with a chicken leg in his hand. "Everyone knew me as Chuck Coleman's son, and everyone expected me to be something special. It was alienating."

Margorie tapped a napkin over her lips. "Nantucket sounds really, really small."

"Too small," Roland agreed, his eyes stormy.

"But you must miss it a little," Margorie tried. "It looks gorgeous in photographs."

"Sure. I miss the water, the beaches, and the hiking." Roland gazed out the window pensively as though there was something else on that list— something he couldn't bring himself to say.

"We didn't have any of that in my hometown," Margorie said. "We just had the grocery store, the gas station, and the diner. And the diner burned down over the summer."

Roland's eyes widened. "And your parents? They're still there?"

Margorie had never told anyone about her difficult relationship with her parents. Even now, with Roland peering across the table at her, fully open to her honesty, she felt stifled.

"They are," Margorie admitted.

"They must miss you," Roland said. "My mother writes me a letter every week."

Margorie's mother hadn't written her anything. But because she wanted to stay in-sync with Roland, she nodded. "Mine, too."

"Weird that Thanksgiving is just two weeks away," Roland said. "This semester was really slow and really fast at the same time."

Margorie hadn't made plans to return home for Thanksgiving. But that evening, when she returned to the female dorms, a sign was taped to the exterior door. It said: DORMS CLOSED FOR THANKSGIVING BREAK. Her stomach tightened with fear. Armed with a new sense of confidence, when she opened the door of her dorm room, she asked Sylvia's boyfriend to leave. When Sylvia made a fuss about it, Margorie insisted she had a headache and crawled into bed with her back facing her. Maybe if she hadn't been given such a crummy roommate, she'd have made more friends by now. Maybe she would have someone to go home with for Thanksgiving.

On the night before Thanksgiving, Margorie boarded a bus and rode out to her tiny town. The night was gray and blue and dense with fog, and she kept her backpack on her lap at all times, her fingers gripping the straps so hard that they turned white. She hadn't told her parents her plan to return, but not for lack of trying. All three times she'd tried to call them this week, the phone had rung and rung without any answer.

Margorie walked a mile from the bus station in the dark cold. When she reached the little house where she'd grown up, she was surprised to find the front windows glowing with orange light. A figure bustled to and fro in the kitchen, her dark red hair streaming out behind her. It was her mother; she was preparing for Thanksgiving. Margorie's heart thudded with recognition.

As usual, the front door wasn't locked. Margorie tiptoed through, eyed her father's sleeping form by the television, dropped her backpack, and ambled into the kitchen. Her mother's back was to her as she swept a rolling pin over a thinning pie crust. Margorie hadn't seen her mother in three months, and she felt a surprise rush of tenderness toward her. She had to hold herself back from running over and throwing her arms around her. They simply weren't that kind of family.

When Margorie took a hesitant step into the kitchen, the floorboards creaked beneath her, and her mother spun on her heel and gaped at her. For a moment, Margorie was terrified she would tell her to go. Instead, a smile burst over her face, and she said, "Oh! My darling girl is home." She then cleared the distance between them and wrapped Margorie in a floury hug.

"I was so hopeful you'd come back!" her mother breathed into her shoulder. "But I didn't think you'd make it."

Margorie melted in her mother's arms. It felt like years since she'd felt any parental love in that house. It was almost as though she'd returned home to a different dimension where the previous rules no longer applied.

"Sit down," her mother instructed. "You must be starving. What can I make you for dinner?"

Margorie sat cross-legged at the kitchen table while her mother put a pot of pasta on the stove and chatted easily about her day and their plans for Thanksgiving. Ten people were coming to the house, and they expected all the fixings, plenty of pie, and an enormous turkey. Margorie's mother showed off the bird in the fridge, where it awaited tomorrow's cooking session.

"Can I help you tomorrow?" Margorie asked as she twirled a fork through her pasta. Red sauce sprinkled back into the bowl as she brought it to her lips.

"I could really use it," her mother said gently. She squeezed Margorie's shoulder and sighed. "I can't tell you how often I've sat in this kitchen over the past few months and wondered how you were. I want to know everything. Everything that's happened to you. You're the first Ratner who ever went to college, you know?"

Margorie was captivated by her mother, who was

unable to look her in the eye. What she said was too heavy with meaning for eye contact.

"What's the best thing you've done?" her mother continued, her voice jagged with oncoming tears. "What have you learned? What have you seen?" She swallowed and finally forced her eyes toward Margorie's, which sent a shiver down Margorie's spine. "You don't have a boyfriend, do you?"

For whatever reason, Roland's face filled Margorie's mind— his sharp cheekbones, his beautiful eyes, and his wild black curls. She hesitated, and her mother's face broke into a smile.

"You do! You're in love. I can see it." Her mother sat at the table beside her and took her hand. "Tell me about him," she urged.

Margorie had never had such power over her mother. She'd never been looked at like this, as though whatever she was about to say was more important than the news or the Bible or the gossip at the local bar.

"What's his name?" her mother whispered. "Just give me that, at least."

Margorie's lips quivered into a smile. "Roland. His name is Roland."

Her mother's face was brighter than the sun. "And what's he like? How did you meet?"

"He's in my literature class," Margorie continued, sensing herself falling down a very dark path. It was terrible to lie, as it meant having to keep track of your lies in the future. "He's brilliant, Mom. You should hear the way he analyzes books. And he genuinely respects what I have to say."

Her mother blinked several times as though she was

unsure of what Margorie meant. "And what do you do together?"

"We do everything together," Margorie said. "We eat together. We go on walks. We watch films."

Her mother pressed her palms together and heaved a sigh. For a long time, she held that pose, gazing at her daughter.

"I just knew things would work out," she said finally. "High school was so hard for you, Margie. And it just broke my heart to watch you struggle. But in Amherst, you've found yourself. And you've found your future husband! Roland."

Margorie's heartbeat skipped. The look on her mother's face was too intense to look at head-on, and the depths of her lie tugged at her. Still, she reminded herself, it wasn't a full-blown lie. She and Roland really did see one another all the time. He was the only person on campus who genuinely cared about her. Perhaps soon, they would accidentally kiss under the stone archway of the literature building or beneath a sprawling campus oak. They were just a few months away from a real relationship. It had to be so.

Chapter Twelve

After Margorie's mother pulled the last pie from the oven, it was past midnight. Margorie's father remained knocked-out in front of the television, his chest rising and falling with his ragged snores. Margorie wished her mother goodnight and tiptoed past him, lugging her backpack on her shoulder all the way to her childhood bedroom. There, she found heaps of her father's hunting supplies— guns and bow and arrows, all piled up where she'd once kept her dolls. Her dolls, it seemed, had been shoved under the bed. She fell to her knees on the brown carpet and brought her dolls out from the darkness one by one, smoothing out the wrinkles of their dresses. Each of them had been hand-me-downs or second-hand, whatever Goodwill had had on the day her mother had decided Margorie was worthy of a new toy. But each of them carried memories of a past Margorie couldn't help but feel nostalgic about. She'd spent hours in her bedroom, pretending her dolls were real, that they were her nearest and dearest friends. She'd told them all of her secrets. When her parents had bickered and screamed in the living room, she'd cried to them, imagining that they cried with her, too.

Very quietly, Margorie whispered, "I met a boy," to them, and she imagined the dolls giggling and asking her for more information. "I'll tell you more tomorrow," Margorie explained as she lined them up on the far end of her bed. At eighteen, she was far too old for dolls, far too old to talk to them. Here in her bedroom, though, nobody could hear her. She was alone. She was safe.

That night, Margorie slept like a rock and awoke to the smells of baking turkey and fresh bread. When she tip-toed to the bathroom, she heard her mother and father's voices in the kitchen.

"She looks great," her mother was saying. "And she said something about a boyfriend."

"A boyfriend, huh?" Margorie's father sounded hungover and sleepy.

"I knew she'd grow out of that awkward spell."

"I'm not so sure about that," her father said, a joke hanging in his voice. "Maybe the boyfriend's just as weird as she is."

"Stop that," her mother scolded, giggling.

Margorie closed the bathroom door behind her and blinked at her reflection in the mirror. Although it was true she'd been an awkward teenager, her teeth bungled up with braces and her acne prolific, she looked genuinely normal these days. Sometimes, she even caught a flash of jealousy in her roommate's eyes when she brushed out her long, red hair. Perhaps her parents couldn't see anything but the strange daughter they'd raised; maybe they'd never see her for what she'd become. Could she ever forgive them for that?

Margorie took a shower and changed into a black

turtleneck and a long skirt. She then steeled herself for her father's rage, set her jaw, and stepped out into the living room. Instead of her father glowering at her, as she was accustomed, she found three of her aunts, an uncle, two cousins, and her father, all watching the Thanksgiving Day Parade from the couch and chairs her father had dragged out of the basement.

"There she is! Our college girl!" Aunt Linda hurried to hug Margorie, bringing with her a wave of putrid perfume.

After a few other hugs, Margorie found herself face-to-face with her father. He sniffed and gave her a once-over as though deciding if she was worthy of his presence. He then said, "What time did you get in last night?"

Margorie considered how to respond. The truth was, she'd returned home far before bedtime. But if she revealed that in front of her family members, proving that her father had been conked out in front of the television due to alcohol, her father would get angry.

"Pretty late," Margorie said. "The bus schedule was messed up."

"You should have picked her up, Randy," Aunt Linda told her father.

"She didn't even tell us she was coming home," her father said.

"She wanted it to be a surprise," Aunt Linda said. "Didn't you, honey?"

Margorie nodded and tried to smile at her father, but he glowered at her and pulled a package of cigarettes from his back pocket.

"I'm going to go help Mom. Anyone need anything?" Margorie stepped around her father and noted the orders from her cousins, aunts, and uncle: a few sodas, some chips and crackers. Margorie breezed into the kitchen to find her mother and her mother's three sisters, all smoking cigarettes and wearing stained aprons.

"There she is!" Aunt Kathy stabbed her cigarette into an ashtray and wagged her eyebrows at Margorie. "Your mother was just telling us about your college boyfriend."

Margorie's heart thumped. She reached for the coffee pot and poured herself a mug as her aunts begged her for more information about the guy. Did she have a photograph? Did he play sports? Why hadn't she invited him home for Thanksgiving?

"It's still new," Margorie explained timidly. She sipped her coffee and tried to smile.

"But I can see it in her eyes," Aunt Kathy assured everyone. "She's in love."

Margorie donned an apron and got to work, helping her mother and aunts with the final sides and fixings required for the one p.m. meal. More and more family members arrived until their little house overflowed.

"I was only expecting ten people!" Margorie's mother laughed and lit another cigarette. "But the more the merrier, I guess."

At one, Margorie's family crammed around three tables stationed across the living room. The television continued to blare the football game, and Margorie's father chewed with his mouth full as he stared at the screen. Margorie sat near her aunts, kitty-corner from her father, and her blood pressure spiked every time one of her mother's sisters brought up Roland. It seemed like a topic they were constantly circling, just as they spoke about the weather or a local shopping sale.

"Does Roland like it when you cook for him?" Aunt Kathy asked.

"And who is Roland?" Aunt Linda demanded from the other side of Margorie's father.

Margorie's father coughed and sputtered into laughter. "Is that your little boyfriend, Margorie?" His eyes were glazed, and he continued to stare at the television.

Linda swatted her brother and rolled her eyes. "No father likes to see his daughter grow up," she assured Margorie.

Margorie's father guzzled his beer, his third or fourth since that morning. Margorie could never shake the habit of counting how many he'd drunk if only to protect herself from his moods. If that was his fourth, they were headed toward dangerous territory.

"She thinks she's something special," her father continued. "Going to college and all that."

The table's mood shifted. Margorie swallowed a lump of mashed potatoes and gravy and stared at her plate.

"Let's not do that, Randy," Aunt Linda tried. "It's Thanksgiving. And your daughter is here! She's visiting. Let's have a nice time, shall we?"

Randy grunted. Margorie was no longer hungry, and she turned to face her mother, wondering if she planned to stand up for her at all. But her mother was preoccupied with her own mashed potatoes, drawing fork lines through the mound.

"Just don't know why she has to come in here and flaunt her new life in front of us," Randy continued. "We gave her everything. Apparently, that wasn't enough."

On television, a football player tore across the field with the ball tucked beneath his arm. Margorie's eyes were heavy with tears, and the table blurred.

"Let's stop that talk now," Aunt Linda urged him. "It's a family dinner, Randy. For crying out loud."

107

Quiet fell over the table, punctuated only with the sound of utensils against plates. Nobody knew what to say. A minute or so later, Randy smacked his fist against the table because of something that had happened in the football game, and everyone leaped with fear.

Margorie needed to wipe her face and blow her nose. If she didn't, she knew her father would glance her way and point out how disgusting she looked. It had happened before. As quietly as she could, Margorie stood from the table and hurried to the bathroom. There, she wiped tears from her face and opened her eyes as wide as they could go, willing the redness to fall away. Maybe she could hide in the kitchen for the rest of the afternoon and into the evening, at least until her father fell asleep in front of the television again. Maybe she could lock her bedroom door and wait till Sunday's bus when she would be able to return safely to campus.

Margorie opened the bathroom door to return to the table. But a dark figure lurked in the hallway, his breath heavy with alcohol and meat. Her father leered at her angrily and playfully in a way that had so often confused her when she'd been younger. She'd wanted his attention so much. But when he'd given it to her in the form of violence, confusion had rattled her.

Margorie couldn't get past him. She was stunned in the doorframe.

"Dad?" Margorie whispered.

Her father shook his head menacingly. "Can't believe you'd come into my house and embarrass me like that."

Margorie swallowed and took a step away from him. She was too terrified to speak.

"Coming in here and telling everyone just how much better you are than us," her father went on. "Talking about your fancy school and your fancy boyfriend." He showed his teeth. "Although the boyfriend thing? I'm having trouble believing."

Margorie winced. Her father noticed.

"Ah! I see it written all over your face," her father went on. "That boyfriend of yours is as real as the Easter Bunny. Admit it."

Margorie furrowed her brow. Still, her tongue was useless.

"What are you? Mute, now? Tell me! Tell me he isn't real!"

The back of Randy's hand rose in the air and just hovered for a moment before he realized what he was about to do, but then he let his hand fall to his side. Margorie stared at her father in disbelief before he grunted, turned around and left for the living room. She hadn't even realized that she was crying until she touched her wet cheeks. The tears were like a waterfall until she finally mopped them up and made her back to the table.

"Randy! Goodness gracious. Your food is getting cold," Aunt Linda said as Randy trounced past the table. When she locked eyes with Margorie, her gaze echoed with empathy. It occurred to Margorie that her father had probably hit Linda in the past. Maybe their own father had hit them, too.

But that didn't change anything for her. As Margorie approached the dining room table, she heard family members talking about the weather again; someone else suggested the mashed potatoes were better this year than they'd been last year; someone else said they couldn't wait for pie.

Margorie couldn't take it. She'd tried her best in that house. She'd even lied to make herself seem more inter-

109

esting and worthy. Instead of sitting back down, she fled to the kitchen and placed her palms on the counter, surrounded by reeking ashtrays and skillets slick with oil. Her thoughts were manic. What could she do? How could she get through this?

And then, the answer echoed from the back of her mind.

Fiery with her own insanity, Margorie threw herself into her bedroom, hunting through closet drawers until she discovered the university directory she'd received at her orientation. There, in black and white letters and numbers, was the name Roland Coleman, along with his address on Nantucket and his phone number. Margorie could have wept, but she was out of tears.

Back in the kitchen, she waited until the Thanksgiving table was rowdy with conversation, then pressed the phone to her ear and dialed Roland's number. It was three in the afternoon, which meant there was a high likelihood Roland's family was seated for dinner, just like hers. She hated to interrupt them. But this was her only hope.

A woman answered the phone after three rings. "Hello! This is the Coleman residence. Happy Thanksgiving!"

The woman's voice was bright and enthusiastic. It demanded nothing from Margorie. It even assumed she was a close friend or family member, as those were the only sorts to call on Thanksgiving Day.

"Hi." Margorie's voice wavered with nerves. "Happy Thanksgiving. Is Roland there, by chance?"

"Oh! Of course." The woman, who was probably Roland's mother, asked Margorie to wait for a moment.

Margorie closed her eyes tightly, praying her father

wouldn't follow her into the kitchen. She tried to imagine Roland's home on Nantucket— a gorgeous dinner table with beautiful Nantucketers, a father who was proud of him, a mother who filled his plate with seconds and thirds. Roland had mentioned he had a little brother named Grant. Probably, Grant was thrilled his brother was home, blowing off his high school friends to hang out with him. Had Roland told Grant about Margorie? Probably not, she supposed. The boys didn't talk about stuff like that.

And then, Roland answered the phone. Margorie was transported back to her university, back to those gorgeous old-world halls and those immersive literary discussions. She was miles and miles away from the murky, cigarette-smelling kitchen in her terrible town.

"Hello?"

"Roland! Hi. It's me. It's Margorie." She hated how meek she sounded.

"Margorie, hey!" He didn't sound confused; he genuinely sounded happy to hear from her. "Happy Thanksgiving."

"Happy Thanksgiving." Margorie swallowed a lump in her throat. "Listen. Um." Margorie's eyes filled with tears again as she realized what she had to say aloud. "My Dad, um. He um."

"Margorie, are you okay?"

Margorie lowered her voice. "My Dad hits me sometimes. And he almost did again. And I don't know what to do."

She said it as simply as she could, as though she spoke about the weather or the football game.

Roland's tone darkened. "Oh, Margorie. I'm so sorry."

Margorie was quiet. She wasn't sure what else to say.

"You need to get out of there," Roland said.

Margorie's knees wavered beneath her. "I don't have anywhere to go."

Roland sounded authoritative, far older than his eighteen years should have allowed. "Listen to me very carefully," he said. "Go pack your bag, walk out the door, and get a hotel room somewhere. Anywhere. I'll pack my bag right now and grab the next ferry."

Margorie's head throbbed with a mix of panic and surprise. Was Roland really coming to save her?

"Do you know what hotel you'll be at?" Roland asked.

Very quietly, Margorie said, "The Hillside Motel is the closest to home. I'll go there."

"Hillside," Roland said. "Okay. I should be there in about four hours. Tell the hotel concierge I'll pay as soon as I get there."

Margorie's eyes stung. "You don't have to do this."

But Roland was resolute. "I'll be there in four hours," he repeated. "Your father can't get away with this. And you shouldn't have to spend Thanksgiving alone."

Chapter Thirteen

It took Margorie five minutes to pack. There, at the door of her childhood bedroom, she took note of everything: the dolls on the bed, the hunting supplies, the cross-stitch of a sailboat on the wall. This was the world she'd been born into; this was where she'd cowered, day and night, praying her father's rage wouldn't find her. But she was an adult now. She had other options. And Roland was coming to save her.

Margorie tip-toed down the hallway with her backpack over her shoulder. In the living room, her father explained what had just happened in the football game to his aunts, who all pretended to care, probably because they were just as afraid of him as Margorie was. When she reached the doorway to the kitchen, she saw her mother hovering over the pie pans with a large knife. It had been a little while since Margorie had seen her father hit her mother. Maybe five or six years. Then again, she hadn't been home since August. Men like Randy needed a punching bag, and Margorie's mother had been the only person around.

Margorie's breathing was ragged, and her cheeks were salty with dried tears. For a moment, she considered walking over to her mother, touching her elbow, and saying, *I'm leaving. Come with me.* But she knew her mother was in too deep. She would make an immediate fuss, tell Margorie she was acting dramatic, and bring her father back in here. Margorie couldn't take it. Before she lost her nerve, she whisked her way toward the foyer, opened the door as softly as she could, and stepped into the sharp chill of the late November afternoon. The door kissed gently to a close, and with that, she was out of the house, out of her family. She couldn't imagine ever returning.

Margorie walked all the way to the motel with her hands shoved deep in her pockets. To distract herself, she thought back to the books she'd read for literature class that semester, Jane Austen and Brontë and H. G. Wells, imagining herself as an English professor somewhere prestigious, like Harvard. Maybe she would make a speech one day about all she'd had to overcome to make it. Maybe she'd thank her father for all the terror he'd brought to her life because it forced her to work that much harder. In this fantasy, Roland was waiting for her just to the left of the stage, maybe carrying their toddler in his arms. "Look at what Mommy did," he'd say. "Look at how good she is."

The man behind the front desk at the motel had skin the color of rotten milk and purple caverns under his eyes. The motel was nearly full due to the influx of family members coming in for the holidays, but he said, "Lucky you. We have one more left." When Margorie said her boyfriend could pay in a few hours, when he got in from Nantucket, the man shrugged and said, "As long as you leave a valuable here behind the desk, you can pay tomorrow morning." Margorie winced. What valuable did she have? She leafed through her wallet and eventually procured her driver's license and a twenty-dollar bill, telling him, "I'm a college student. This money is much more important to me than I can fully explain." He told her this would suffice and placed a thick iron key on the counter. "Room seven."

The motel room was simple and clean. The double-bed was stiff; the carpeting was dark brown and plush, and the bathroom had blue tile and a large mirror. Margorie's reflection scared her. She looked both like a little girl and an older woman, her hair stringy, her face blotchy. Probably, people who looked like her, upset and at the end of their rope, checked into the motel all the time. She suddenly had a hunch she wasn't going to get that twenty-dollar bill back.

Margorie sat at the edge of the bed and fell back, splaying her arms on either side of her. It had been only an hour since she'd called Roland on the phone. If he got out the door on time, that meant she only had to wait three hours. Three hours till Roland appeared at her doorstep and wrapped his strong arms around her. Three hours till he said: "That shouldn't have happened to you, and it never will again."

Then again, what if Roland's parents didn't let him go? Would Margorie wait there all night, only to be unable to pay tomorrow? And what did she think she would do then?

Margorie hadn't eaten much from her Thanksgiving dinner, and her stomach shifted uncomfortably with hunger. She rummaged through her backpack, looking for snacks that she never found. When she retreated outside, she found a vending machine, where she purchased a Hershey's bar that she tore open immediately. The chocolate melted on her tongue, and she closed her eyes at the influx of sugar. When she returned to her room, however, she realized that in her haste, she'd forgotten her key. The man at the front desk giggled at her when she slunk back for help. "You're having a great Thanksgiving, aren't you?" he tried to joke.

A knock rang out on the hotel door at ten-thirty that night— many, many hours after Margorie's phone call to Nantucket. By this point, she'd fallen into a drizzly sleep, and she'd drooled all over her pillow. *Jane Eyre* was open on the opposite pillow, the only book she'd brought home with her because she was due to write a paper on it soon. For some reason, she assumed the person who'd knocked on the door was her father, that he'd figured out where she was, that he was prepared to drag her home by the hair.

Margorie opened the door to find Roland standing there. Snow breezed across his face and melted against his coat, and his cheeks were bright red from the chill.

"Margorie," he said. "I'm so sorry. I'm late."

Margorie was still soft with sleep. She stepped back and beckoned for him to enter, and he did, dropping his backpack off to the side and unzipping his coat. After spending so many hours alone in the hotel room, the weight and shadow of a full man terrified Margorie. But the sight of his face, a face she'd come to love, helped her breathe.

"I didn't think you were coming," Margorie said quietly.

Roland nodded and rubbed the snow from his hair. "I missed the ferry and had to get the very last one. The phone at the ferry office was out, and I wasn't sure how to get a hold of your hotel, anyway."

Margorie nodded. It was all explainable. She just couldn't believe he'd made it.

"Oh, Margorie," Roland said, stepping forward and frowning. "I can't believe that your dad almost hit you."

Margorie looked down at the carpet, embarrassed.

"It's nothing new. I've had to live with this monster my entire life. This time, for some reason, he walked away," Margorie said quietly. "But I've never questioned it before. Today, though, something came over me. And I just couldn't live with it."

Roland's eyes were stormy. He collapsed on the edge of the bed and rubbed his face with his hands. "I wish you would have told me. I would have invited you home for Thanksgiving."

Margorie's heart hammered. Would it really have been so simple?

"I guess I hoped he would be different this time," Margorie offered. "That he would see me as this college student who was worthy of his respect."

Roland nodded. In the silence, Margorie stepped forward and dropped herself on the edge of the mattress beside him. Never in her life had she shared a bed with another man, yet, due to the lateness of the hour, they would need to. This was a terrifying thrill, which contradicted the horror of the rest of the day. She felt as though she and Roland were like bandits, up against the world.

"I can't thank you enough for coming," Margorie whispered.

Roland removed his shoes and shifted up onto the bed to lean against the headboard. Margorie followed his lead so that they were like a husband and wife, chatting in bed at the end of a long day.

"To be honest with you," Roland said, "I wasn't having a very good Thanksgiving. I was happy to get away."

Margorie shifted so that she faced him. She imagined pressing her head against his chest and listening to his heartbeat.

"What happened?" Margorie asked.

"It's nothing compared to what happened to you," Roland said. "I feel bad even bringing it up."

"It's not a competition," Margorie assured him. "If you want to talk about it, I'm here."

Roland tugged at his hair. "I feel like I'm in a free-fall right now. Like I don't know myself anymore."

Margorie furrowed her brow. She'd never heard Roland talk like this before.

"For the past four years, I've been in a serious relationship," Roland explained, his voice like a string. "We had all these plans, you know. We got into the same university. We wanted to move into an apartment together and study for grad school. She's much smarter than me, of course. Her future is bright."

A shiver of jealousy fell down Margorie's spine.

"But this past summer, her mom got sick, and her dad left," Roland went on. "She got bogged down, caring for her mother and making money for them both. I sensed there was something wrong, but I ignored it, choosing to believe our future was still intact. But not long before we were supposed to leave, she told me she wasn't going with me."

Margorie's heart shattered at the edges. It seemed

impossible that anyone had ever been allowed to love Roland before her.

"She asked me not to reach out to her," Roland went on, "and I gave her plenty of space the past couple of months. But this morning, I couldn't take it anymore, and I went over to her house. All the windows were dark, but there was a car in the driveway. I banged on the door, but nobody answered. To add insult to injury, I found out my Aunt Jessabelle has been working with her at the library for the past few months— but she won't tell me anything about her. She won't even tell me if she's doing okay. Gosh, it riled me up." Roland punched his thigh, his face scrunched up.

Margorie hated to see Roland in so much pain. More than that, she hated that it was another woman who'd caused that pain. Still, she reminded herself Roland's ex-girlfriend wasn't here in the hotel room. That was Margorie. Margorie would help him through.

"I know it sounds stupid," Roland went on. "Everyone breaks up after high school. I get that. But I just never imagined Estelle and I would."

The name "Estelle" echoed in Margorie's head after that. It was a deliriously beautiful name, exotic and French. Margorie felt like a farmer in comparison.

"My entire life, until the past few months, was about Estelle," Roland went on. "And I'm just trying to figure out a new idea for myself."

Margorie wondered if this was her opening. Maybe this was when she was supposed to throw herself on top of Roland and profess her love. But the look in his eyes was too painful. This wasn't the moment. They were two lost souls in a motel room. That was all.

Although nothing happened that night, Margorie had never felt closer to another human in her life. She lay there deep into the night, listening to Roland's soft breathing, sometimes taking furtive glances at his naked back, which was greenish in the soft parking lot light that came in through either side of the curtains. Margorie hardly allowed herself to think of her father and mother at home. Probably, her father was too drunk to even consider her absence. Her mother was probably smoking her fiftieth cigarette, talking about Margorie's new boyfriend, her new start. Margorie reminded herself that, in order to build a life, you had to take a step in a brand-new direction. She couldn't let the past define her.

Chapter Fourteen

Present Day

It was the first year of the Aquinnah Cliffside Overlook Hotel Christmas Party – an event that would eventually become a much-beloved annual event. Daniel explained the importance of the affair over coffee one chilly morning at the bookstore, using his hands to articulate the beauty and the rage of the old hotel. "It was destroyed in a hurricane in 1943," he said, "and reopened just this past summer. It still captures the old-world charm of the original place, even down to the intricate painting across the ceiling. You have to see it."

Apparently, Daniel had been invited to the Christmas party because the current owner, Kelli Montgomery, was a regular at the bookstore. "She reads just about everything," he explained as he shelved books happily. "Detective stories, romances, fantasy. Anything I throw at her, she reads voraciously."

"Doesn't she have too many responsibilities at the

hotel?" Margorie had heard hoteliers were victims of twenty-four-hour jobs, ones that often led to burn-out.

"She did," Daniel said. "But when she felt herself losing her mind, she delegated."

"I can't imagine working with so many people," Margorie said.

"Writers always say that." Daniel smiled, his dimples sharp dark dots. "But you seem like a people person to me."

"Do I?" Margorie had never in her life felt like a people person. Her husband, Tom, had had to drag her out to parties and give her pep-talks before holidays spent with his family.

"We met each other in public," Daniel said. "And you didn't recoil when I sat down with you."

"I think that's the first time that's happened." Margorie smiled, unable to resist Daniel's charms.

Daniel finished shelving books and swept across the bookstore toward the little kiosk, where he sold coffee, hot chocolate, and baked goods. Margorie watched him, amazed at how normal being with him felt. Normally, she felt like an outlier, as though she'd been born with three heads and should have been researched in a lab. He removed a chocolate chip cookie from behind the counter. "Do you like cookies?"

"Who doesn't like cookies?" Margorie asked.

Daniel grabbed a second for himself and filled two cups with coffee. After the temperatures had plummeted outside, no Vineyard residents had braved the streets, and Daniel admitted he was thinking about closing early for the afternoon.

"But not until you tell me you'll go to the Christmas

party with me," he said, dipping a corner of his cookie into the coffee.

Margorie laughed. "You really want me to go?"

"Why not? I'm sure you have plenty of beautiful dresses," Daniel said. "Why not bring one of them out of the back of your closet and join me?"

Margorie took a bite of dough and melted chocolate, closing her eyes against the luxury. Daniel had said he ordered the cookies from a sister-baking team across the island named Maggie and Alyssa Potter. Maggie partially owned the other bookstore, The Dog-Eared Corner, and provided similar baked goods to that space— resulting in Daniel's jealousy and ordering of his own batch.

"It's hard to believe you spent so many years away," Margorie said. "You're such an islander."

"They've accepted me back into the fold," Daniel agreed. "It's hard to believe it was so easy. I'm thankful."

The Christmas Party at the Aquinnah Cliffside Overlook Hotel was set for Saturday, December 17th. That was just three days away. Despite Daniel's belief that Margorie had numerous beautiful dresses in her closet, everything she tried on when she returned home after the bookstore either made her look frumpy or out of style or both. In the mirror, she set her jaw and made a plan: she had to go shopping. If she was attending an iconic party on the cliffside of a swanky island resort, she couldn't look like "Margorie Ratner," the little girl who'd come from nothing. She had to look like the gorgeous and successful Margorie Tomlinson. And that required a perfect dress.

Margorie spent all day Thursday shopping. She drove

from boutique to boutique, frowning at herself in the mirrors of dressing rooms, trying to describe her vision to various salesclerks. When she walked into the vintage clothing shop at the tail-end of the day, she had no hope whatsoever. Vintage clothing wasn't her thing.

But when the young woman behind the front desk told her that she owned the shop with her mother, Kelli Montgomery, Margorie's ears perked up. "Kelli Montgomery! I'm going to a party of hers this weekend. That's what the dress is for."

The young woman introduced herself as Lexi Montgomery and explained that she, too, had struggled to find a dress for the party. "But I think I have something perfect for you."

Lexi went into the back, where she procured a dark red dress with a deep V-neck and a slit up the thigh. It was a little scandalous for Margorie's taste, but Lexi urged her to try it on.

"With your skin tone, this dress will come alive," she said. "The woman who dropped it off said she never wore it." In a low tone, Lexi added, "And it's designer."

Margorie stepped into the dressing room and donned the dress, avoiding her reflection. But when she stepped back into the store, flipping her red hair behind her, Lexi's jaw dropped.

"Look!" Lexi beckoned for the three-way mirror, where Margorie was featured. The dress made her thighs, sculpted from years of yoga, look longer than they ever had. Her bare shoulders glistened, and her waist looked sleek and thinner than it had since her fifties.

"This has got to be a magic dress," Margorie breathed. "There's no other explanation."

When she returned to her beach house, Margorie

hung the dress in her closet and sat at the edge of her bed for a long time, watching the snow flicker down on the other side of her bedroom window. When she checked the clock on the bedside table, she was surprised to note she'd lost nearly an hour in daydreaming. Something had taken over her mind ever since she'd met Daniel. She was constantly lost in thought.

Daniel picked her up for the Christmas party at six-thirty Saturday evening. Beforehand, Margorie had taken the entire afternoon to shower, lotion, do her makeup, and style her hair. Nobody could say looking and staying beautiful wasn't hard work. But as she swept down the porch steps to meet Daniel, the look in his eyes as he got out of the car was worth all the work.

"Margorie..." He trailed off as though words them-selves had lost all meaning for him. "You look remarkable."

Margorie blushed and dropped her gaze to the sharp stretch of white snow between them. Her heart ballooned. After another moment's pause, Daniel remem-bered himself and cut around the car to open the passenger door. He then pressed a kiss onto her cheek so as not to mess up her red lipstick.

On the drive to the Aquainnah Cliffside Overlook Hotel, Daniel and Margorie returned to their easy banter. Daniel told her about a song he'd just heard on the radio, one he couldn't get out of his head, and as he spoke about it, the radio station played the song yet again. Daniel howled, "No! Make it stop!" as Margorie sang along. "I don't think it's half as bad as you do," she teased.

Daniel's cheeks were red from laughter as he pulled into the hotel parking lot, which was already full. As they strode toward the hotel, Margorie took a moment to see the grand mansion for what it was— something drawn from the dramatic history of the island. It was regal, the closest the island had to a castle. As they drew closer to the front door, the sound of 1920s' Big Band music floated through the chilly air.

"It really feels like we traveled through time," she said.

In the foyer of the hotel, the manager, a woman named Piper, approached to greet them and direct them toward the coatroom. As Margorie unfurled her coat from her shoulders, Daniel's eyes traced her naked shoulders and the way her hair fell across her back. Margorie had been around the block a few times; she was no longer Margorie Ratner, a girl without experience who didn't understand where she fit in society. She'd become a beautiful woman, and she was proud of that.

Sometimes, Margorie remembered her mother's beauty. She'd been the prettiest girl at her small-town high school, the object of affection for every teenage boy. For some reason, Randy Ratner had scooped her up and changed her life. And Margorie's mother had paid the price for that decision every day of her life.

The ballroom featured a wide array of islanders, many of whom Daniel knew one way or another. They wore glittering dresses and tuxedos and drank cocktails in colors of burnt orange and dark brown. Daniel introduced Margorie to several women with the last name of Sheridan, all with long, glinting brunette waves, then to a woman named Oriana, who worked as an art dealer across Nantucket, Martha's Vineyard, and New York City.

"She's sold some very well-known pieces," Daniel said as they stepped away from Oriana. "But wait till I tell you the story of the three-million-dollar art forgery she sold by accident."

Margorie's eyes widened. "Do tell!"

"Later." Daniel chuckled. "I can see you're a writer. Your mind is already awash with potential stories."

Margorie laughed and sipped her negroni cocktail. She still hadn't told Daniel she hadn't written a book in more than five years, that the idea of sitting alone with her thoughts in front of a computer terrified her.

A part of the ballroom was portioned off for slow dancing. From the sidelines, Margorie watched the couples sway, their eyes locked as they spoke in soft tones. Many of the couples were her age or older, couples who'd gone through the textures of time together. A stab in her gut reminded her that she should have been able to have that with Tom.

"Would you like to dance?" Daniel asked quietly.

Margorie swallowed another gulp of the sharp cocktail. "I'd like that very much."

When they finished their drinks, Daniel led Margorie to the ballroom floor, placed his hand along the small of her back, and took her smaller hand in his. Although Margorie was anxious and jittery, she forced herself to look Daniel in the eye. She was enthralled with the magic of him. He seemed taken directly from one of the books she'd written twenty years ago. Oh, her heart already ached with what could be love for him. But it was too soon, wasn't it? She had to hold herself back. She had to be careful.

After the song petered out, Margorie took her hand away from his and slid it through her hair. "Let's get another drink," she suggested. The intensity on the floor was too much for her.

Daniel grabbed two more cocktails from the bar, and they stood near a painted window, watching guests and chatting about anything that came to their mind. A formidable woman, slightly taller than most other women at the party, entered with a handsome man in a tuxedo. There was an air to them both, as though they had money and knew how to spend it.

"There's Kelli!" Daniel waved toward the woman, who immediately brightened upon seeing him. "She and her fiancé, Xander Van Tress, own the place."

Margorie furrowed her brow. "That's Xander Van Tress?" She'd heard about him across New England. He often purchased old property like this and flipped it. It was strange to see him in the flesh.

"Daniel! I'm so glad you could make it." Kelli wrapped Daniel in a hug, then stepped back and smiled earnestly at Margorie. A split-second later, her eyes lit up with recognition. "No way! I know you! Xander, this is Margorie Tomlinson!"

Daniel touched Margorie's lower back for support. "This is my date," he said proudly. "I suppose she's a celebrity!"

"You very much are," Kelli said, taking Margorie's hand and raising it slowly. "I've read all of your books. Some of them multiple times. I'm sure you hear this from so many of your fans, but you've gotten me through some dark times."

Margorie's cheeks burned. "Thank you so much for saying that."

Kelli's eyes glinted, and she dropped Margorie's hand. From behind her came the sound of her name, and she made a face and said, "I have to run. But I want to pick your brain later. If you have the time?"

"I'm not going anywhere," Margorie assured her. "Thank you so much for the party. It's gorgeous."

"Margorie Tomlinson likes my party!" Kelli smiled. "It's too good to be true."

Kelli and Xander hurried back through the crowd, leaving Daniel and Margorie alone.

"Does that embarrass you?" Daniel asked after a moment. "When people recognize you, I mean."

Margorie raised her shoulders. "In some ways, of course. But I try to remember my old life. I came from nothing. All I had were my dreams of getting out of there, away from my father. And I always wanted to become a writer."

"And you did it."

Margorie waved her hand. "I need to remember to be grateful."

Soon afterward, waiters and waitresses in ornate uniforms straight from the 1920s ambled through the crowd with trays of salmon puffs, canapés, bruschetta, and miniature soft pretzels. The food was exquisite and flavorful, proof that whatever chef lurked in the kitchen of the Aquinnah was worth whatever they paid him. After another few snacks, Margorie allowed Daniel to take her back out onto the ballroom floor, where they swayed gently and gazed into one another's eyes some more. Margorie had begun to ask herself whether or not she would allow Daniel to stay over at her beach house one of these days. Why did the thought of that terrify her so much? She was seventy years old! Shouldn't she be too old for such fear?

Five songs later, Margorie admitted she was tired and needed another drink. They returned to the bar, where they chatted with Susan Sheridan and her husband, Scott

Frampton, about their family's inn, the Sunrise Cove, and Susan's daughter's pregnancy. When Margorie said she was a writer, Susan made no indication of knowing her. "I read mostly legal texts and legal thrillers," Susan admitted. "But maybe I should make more time for romance in my life?"

As they chatted, Kelli Montgomery returned, her eyes glinting.

"I see you've met my cousin," she said of Susan. "Susan, Margorie is one of my favorite writers."

"Wow." Susan smiled. "What a treat for you!"

Kelli nodded. "I've been dying to return to our conversation all night," she began. "For weeks, I've felt so confused about this Estelle Coleman business. I wanted to ask you about it."

Margorie's stomach twisted into knots, and her smile fell immediately. The music was suddenly too loud, almost deafening.

"Beg your pardon?" Margorie asked.

"Estelle Coleman is another romance writer," Kelli explained to Susan and Daniel. "Although I've been a Margorie Tomlinson fan for much longer, I also count myself an Estelle Coleman fan." She returned her gaze to Margorie's. "And the two of you are in a pretty hefty feud right now. It's been a storm in the romance community, to say the least."

"Intriguing!" Susan's eyes widened.

"She stole my story idea," Margorie explained flatly. "It really rattled me. I suppose I stupidly thought you could trust everyone in the romance writing community."

"How terrible," Susan said. "Let me know if you need a lawyer."

Kelli furrowed her brow. "But that's the thing," she

offered. "I've read your book, *A Christmas Dream*, multiple times. I love it. So, so much. But I've also read her book, *A Bright Christmas*. And yes, I see the similarities. They're both Christmas romances about two people coming back together after separations. But beyond that?" Kelli shrugged. "I guess I don't really get the legality of it all. Like, what she published doesn't seem like a copy at all. But I'm also not a writer. What do I know?"

Margorie's lips parted with shock. She felt as though she'd just been smacked in public.

"Copyright law is complicated," Susan said with a smile.

"Completely," Kelli went on, waving her hand. "How is it going? Do you think you'll go to court?" She seemed not to know how much she'd upset Margorie, which was a good thing.

"We're still in the early stages," Margorie stuttered. "Like you said, it's complicated." She drained the rest of her glass and twitched her head away. "I have to find the bathroom. Can you point me in the right direction?"

"Of course." Kelli gave her directions, which Margorie didn't listen to at all. She thanked her and sped away from Daniel, through the pulsing crowd, and down the nearest hallway, where she placed her forehead against the cool wall and focused on her breathing. In and out. In and out. She couldn't believe the nerve of that woman, Kelli. She couldn't believe she'd called her out like that.

But what if she was right? The thought rang through Margorie's mind and gave her pause. Before she could fully take stock of that notion, however, Daniel called for her from the end of the hallway. Margorie couldn't breathe. She turned slowly to find him running toward her, his face scrunched with worry.

"Are you all right?" Daniel asked, his hand over his chest.

Margorie grimaced as she searched Daniel's eyes for his judgment. He was friends with Kelli, which meant he probably took what she'd said to heart.

"I'm just really tired," Margorie said, although she'd never been more awake in her life.

Daniel looked deflated. "Do you want a cup of coffee or something?"

"No." Margorie tugged her hair. "I'm going to call a cab and head home."

"I can drive you," Daniel said.

"No," Margorie insisted. "You're here with your friends. It's a fabulous party. I don't want to ruin it for you."

Daniel stuttered with surprise. Their gorgeous, romantic evening together had combusted.

"Did I do something wrong?" Daniel asked sheepishly.

Margorie wanted to burst into tears. She wanted to press him against the wall and hug him tightly until her arms ached with the weight of how much she wanted to be understood. She felt like an embarrassment unto herself, someone not worthy of his nor anyone's love.

"You were wonderful," Margorie said, her voice breaking.

"Then stay. Stay with me."

Margorie shook her head. "I wish I could. But I really can't." She then whisked around him and hurried to coat check as tears filled her eyes. She felt terribly stupid. Out at the edge of the parking lot, she shivered in her coat, watching for the bright yellow of a taxi to appear at the far end of the very long driveway. Just thirty or so feet away was the jagged edge of the Aquinnah Cliffside, beyond which was the frothing, dark ocean. There, alone in the darkness, Margorie remembered that Thanksgiving night so long ago when she'd walked in the cold all the way to the Hillside Motel to wait for Roland. She should have known, then, that she was destined, ultimately, to be alone.

Chapter Fifteen

That Sunday afternoon, Estelle and Roland hosted their family for dinner. From the kitchen, where she stirred a large pot of mashed potatoes, watching the butter melt and ooze through the creamy texture, Estelle listened to her massive family swap stories and crack jokes, compliment the Christmas tree, and laugh with one another. Despite how bruised her heart felt and how achy she was after losing her publishing contract and numerous fans, Estelle reminded herself to count her blessings. All of her family was under one roof. They were safe.

"Grandma! Hey!" Rachelle and Darcy appeared in the doorway, Rachelle in a Christmassy red dress and Darcy in a velvet black sweater and a pair of jeans.

"Hello, my girls." Estelle turned to hug them. "Are there enough snacks out there for you?"

"Plenty," Rachelle assured her. "Do you need any help in here?"

Estelle glanced around the kitchen, stocked with

baked apple, pumpkin, and pecan pies, bubbling pots, and huge trays of food waiting for their turn to be warmed up in the oven. Hilary and Samantha were out in the garage, fetching wine and beer; when they returned, Estelle had another list of things for them to do.

"I think your mother, Aunt Hilary, and I have it all covered," Estelle said. "Thank you."

Rachelle blushed and removed her phone from her dress pocket. "We have something to show you. If you have time?"

Estelle furrowed her brow and dried her hands on a kitchen towel. Rachelle and Darcy watched her expectantly as Rachelle turned the phone around.

"What am I looking at?" Estelle asked them, blinking at a series of photographs of her own romance novels.

"We made a TikTok channel for you!" Rachelle announced. "And you already have fifty-thousand followers!"

"People follow you like crazy," Darcy explained. "It's partially due to the feud, of course."

"But also, there are so many romance readers on TikTok," Rachelle continued. "They're huge fans of yours, and they want to be connected to you in any way they can be."

Estelle had heard of TikTok in an abstract way. "You made videos of my books? I just don't understand."

"Just short ones," Darcy said, glancing at Rachelle nervously. "Our plan was to build your network so that you could eventually post a video of your own."

"I don't know anything about making videos," Estelle said, her voice wavering.

"We can help you," Rachelle said.

"We thought maybe your fans would want to hear from you," Darcy offered quietly. "You could explain what's happening with Margorie Tomlinson— and even tell everyone that *A Bright Christmas* is based on your real life."

"In your own words," Rachelle finished and nodded furiously.

In their eyes, Estelle saw reflected back their love and tremendous hard work, all in pursuit of clearing Estelle's name. It was the most beautiful thing her grandchildren had ever done for her. And she didn't have the heart to refute it.

"We can try," Estelle said at last. "Maybe after dinner?"

A moment later, Hilary and Samantha burst into the kitchen, laden with wine and beer. Rachelle and Darcy got to work setting the table for the upcoming feast. Estelle flew around the kitchen and dining room, her heart pounding with worry for this upcoming video. She had very little experience speaking on camera. And what if, in speaking to her "fans," they found something they didn't like about her? What if they turned on her even more?

After dinner, Sam and Hilary shooed Estelle away from the clean-up, telling her she'd done enough. Feeling like a child who'd gotten in trouble, Estelle followed Rachelle and Darcy upstairs to her study, where they closed the door behind them and considered how to set up the shot. To distract herself from her sorrows, Estelle had put a small Christmas tree in the study, decorated with glinting lights and ornaments from her own child-hood. One of them was a small porcelain doll that had belonged to her mother, Carrie, when she'd been very small. As Rachelle and Darcy squabbled about how to light the room for the video, Estelle reached out to touch the doll's porcelain hair. Oh, how she missed her mother. Especially around Christmas.

Finally, Darcy and Rachelle decided where to put Estelle's work chair— directly beside the Christmas tree, where the Christmas tree lights could illuminate Estelle's face. Estelle sat and placed her chin on her fist as Rachelle situated her phone on a tripod they'd apparently brought from home.

"This seems a little involved for an internet video," Estelle said with a laugh.

"It has to look slightly professional, Grandma," Rachelle explained. "If I hold it, the camera will jiggle around. Nobody wants to see that."

"I'm glad to have you both here," Estelle said softly, straightening her spine.

"Do you know what you're going to say?" Darcy asked.

Estelle furrowed her brow. She'd hoped ideas would flow freely through her mind and out of her mouth, but nerves had begun to bubble in her stomach, and she wasn't sure of anything anymore. "I think so," she lied.

"We can do a few different takes," Rachelle said. "Ready?"

Estelle nodded and blinked at Rachelle's phone, suddenly petrified. She remembered the first moment she'd ever heard about this supposed plagiarism, how naked she'd felt in front of all those people in New York City. Had Margorie meant to be so cruel to her? Had Margorie meant to ruin her career?

"Grandma," Rachelle said, stopping the video. "Are you okay?"

Estelle blinked back tears. "I'm sorry. I guess I wasn't ready after all."

"It's okay," Darcy assured her.

"Remember, this is your chance to set the record straight," Rachelle said.

Estelle sniffed and set her jaw. Rachelle was right. She had to stand up for herself. She couldn't lose the fans she'd grown to love over the past decade.

When Rachelle hit the play button on the video, Estelle raised her chin and spoke, pretending that she chatted with a dear friend or a close confidant.

"Hello," she began, "and Merry Christmas from the island of Nantucket. It's here in this office that I've written all of my books over the years. It's here I've dreamed up my stories for all of you. I've been so grateful for your feedback and your loyalty over the years. It was always my wildest dream to become a writer, and the fact that it's happened is something that will eternally mystify me."

Estelle swallowed. Rachelle nodded, urging her on.

"I wanted to address the recent allegations against me," Estelle went on, her voice wavering. "When I first learned that a fellow romance writer accused me of plagiarizing, I was flabbergasted. I genuinely respect this other writer and have even met her several times at romance writing conventions. I had hoped she respected me enough to think I would never do something like this. But alas. We can't always control what other people think of us, can we?

"*A Bright Christmas*, my most recent novel, is based on a very strange time of my life," Estelle continued. "I was eighteen at the time and very lonely, nursing my mother

back to health here on Nantucket. The events that tran-
spired around Christmas of that year, 1971, are near and
dear to my heart, and I always wanted to put them into a
book. *A Bright Christmas* is that very book." Estelle's eyes
misted with tears that she quickly blinked away. "I hate that
Margorie Tomlinson feels I copied her. I hate it so much.
But I can't do anything about what she thinks. All I can do
is stand by my work and hope that all of you, my fans, stand
by me, too. Thank you all, and Merry Christmas."

Rachelle snapped off the video and burst to her feet
with applause. Darcy followed her lead as Estelle fell
forward and placed her face in her hands. Her adrenaline
was spiking.

"That was perfect, Grandma," Rachelle assured her.
"I'm going to post it, okay?"

Estelle raised her shoulders. "Okay. Go ahead."
Secretly, she was petrified.

Downstairs, Hilary greeted her with a glass of merlot
and presented her with the prime seat in the living room
directly next to the crackling fire. Her family played
charades in two teams, and Charlie was currently up,
imitating something the opposite team had to guess. He
wagged his arms foolishly, and everyone erupted with
laughter.

Rachelle sat cross-legged next to Estelle and passed
over her cell phone. "Look," she said. "It already has three
thousand views! And so many people have liked it and
commented."

As Charlie continued to dance and gesture around
the living room, Estelle pored over the comments from
her fans.

Minniemouse779 said: I always knew you

were wonderful, Estelle. Thank you for being you.

Jemima929 said: I don't get what all the fuss is about. A Bright Christmas and A Christmas Dream are totally different!

"I can't believe this," Estelle breathed. But just then, she spotted several more comments, none of which believed her.

LanaDelJankow said: You need to unpublish your book and issue an apology. Now.

HannahViolet said: I hate when people make excuses like this. Grow up, Estelle.

Estelle grimaced and passed the phone back to Rachelle. "Not everyone believes me."

"That's the nature of the internet, Grandma," Rachelle said, touching her knee. "I think it's good you put yourself out there. You're facing this head-on."

But later that night, Estelle couldn't sleep. She sat up in the darkness of her bedroom, where the moonlight spilled in through the window and drenched Roland in light. He was sound asleep, facing away from her. All she wanted was to wrap her body around his warmth and fall into his dream. It seemed silly that so many technological advancements had occurred in modern society, but they still hadn't figured out how you could dream with the person you loved.

Estelle got up and wandered back to her study. There, she did something her lawyer had been telling her not to do: she pulled up Margorie's website again.

And this time, she wrote Margorie an email and actually sent it.

Dear Margorie,

My lawyer has told me not to reach out to you, but I can't take it anymore.

I hate that this is happening. I hate that we can't talk this out. Please tell me where you are. I'll come to you, and we can talk about this face-to-face.

Estelle Coleman

Chapter Sixteen

1971

It was the Saturday after Thanksgiving, and Estelle hadn't slept more than a wink in what felt like days. As she slumped through the front doors of the library, Jessabelle beelined for her with a mug of steaming coffee, which she pressed into her hand. "Why don't you shelve books upstairs today?" Jessabelle suggested tenderly. Estelle was grateful for this. Given that it was a Saturday after a holiday, very few people would probably come in today; even fewer of those people would make an effort to go upstairs. She wanted to be alone.

"How was your Thanksgiving?" Estelle asked shakily as Jessabelle began to walk away.

Jessabelle raised her shoulders. "It was fine. Just ate too much, as usual."

Had she seen Roland? Had Roland told Jessabelle what he'd done? No. It was too embarrassing to say aloud, maybe.

"Let me know if you need anything upstairs," Jessabelle urged her. "Don't work too hard and go home whenever you need to."

Estelle thanked her and slumped up the staircase, only to fall to her knees in front of the bookshelf, her heart pounding. It had been a horrific week.

Estelle's mother had taken a turn the weekend before Thanksgiving, either vomiting or weeping on an endless repeat, and Estelle had had to take a leave of absence from the restaurant to stay home with her. Luckily, Jessabelle had assured her she would put Estelle on the schedule at the library as much as she needed. "Quit the restaurant," Jessabelle urged. "You're needed here."

For the rest of Jessabelle's life, Estelle would never find a way to properly repay her for all her help. Estelle owed her everything.

On Thanksgiving morning, Estelle had had the gall to think she could make herself and her mother a small lunch, at least. But her mother had been very sick and miserable, unable to go far from bed. Exhausted, Estelle had abandoned her half-prepared meal in the kitchen and fallen asleep on the living room couch with the television on. The parade carried on in New York City, floats decorated with cartoon characters and dancers kicking their legs as though the world wasn't about to end. As though the rules of the universe hadn't been tipped on their head.

At some point in the early afternoon came the rap of a fist against the door. Estelle was too groggy to move her head much. Who could it be? Couldn't they leave her alone?

And then, she'd heard it: "Estelle? Are you there? Estelle?" It was Roland, and the sound of his voice sent a shiver down her spine. After hearing that voice every single day for years, it had turned into a source of horror.

Estelle curled into a tight ball and prayed that Roland would get the hint. She couldn't see him, not now; more than that, she couldn't allow him to see her like this. She hadn't washed her hair in several days; she'd hardly eaten lately, resulting in a skeletal look Jessabelle had worried over. After nearly fifteen minutes of knocking and crying her name, Roland finally got the hint. The sound of his motor before his car rocketed away sent Estelle into hysterics. She sobbed into the couch pillow, which still reeked of cigarette smoke, even though her father had left months ago.

Now that it was two days after Thanksgiving, Estelle had to admit something: she'd secretly been waiting for Roland to come back to her door and try again. This time, she told herself, she would answer it. This time, she would throw herself in his arms and tell him she wasn't strong enough to handle this alone. She'd thought she could. She'd been so wrong.

But Roland hadn't been back. And, she knew, he had classes on Monday, which meant he was probably already planning to return to Amherst tomorrow. Oh, she burned with the desire to know what his parents thought of the breakup. Did Chuck secretly champion it because Estelle's last name had never been worthy of the Coleman name? Did Margaret ask about the girls he was seeing in college?

Estelle hadn't known what to do when Roland had come by her house on Thanksgiving. But in not answering the door, she now saw what she'd done. She'd killed them, once and for all. And she had to deal with that.

Jessabelle came upstairs to check on her that afternoon to find that, embarrassingly, Estelle had only shelved half of the books she'd planned to. Jessabelle didn't give her a hard time. Instead, she sat across from her on the floor between bookshelves, crossed her legs beneath her, and said, "How are you holding up?"

Estelle's chin quivered. "I wish I knew how to answer that question."

Jessabelle nodded. There was no judgment in her eyes, only empathy. "Have you written anything down?"

Estelle remembered, with dull embarrassment, that she'd thrown the *How to Write a Novel* book under her bed months ago. She'd never retrieved it.

"I can barely think clearly, let alone write," Estelle admitted.

Jessabelle clasped her knees. "I know you're suffering," she said. "And I know you feel very alone in that."

Estelle dropped her chin and stared at her hands. They seemed so useless to her. When was the last time she'd even written down a grocery list, let alone written down a solitary thought?

"I feel so tired," Estelle offered.

"Can you try writing about that?" Jessabelle suggested. "Don't put pressure on yourself. Just open your heart up and let it flow."

Estelle still felt resistant to the idea, even hours later, when she lay back in bed listening to the November winds blast against her little house. Down the hallway, her mother slept fitfully, coughing herself to bits.

At midnight, Estelle reached under her bed to find *How to Write a Novel*. It was coated with dust, which she smeared off with a towel. Thinking to herself, *"Here goes nothing,"* she opened to the first page and began to read.

Even as she read through the introduction, which spoke about the grand history of novel-writing in the previous centuries, Estelle felt heavy with doubt. There was no way she could write something as dense and as beautiful as her favorite novels. There was no way she could demand others to read her prose alone in their rooms across the United States, wading through the imagined worlds of her mind.

But still, she kept reading. Perhaps in learning to write, she would teach herself to think properly again. And perhaps, somewhere in that process, she would find a way to heal. Maybe.

Chapter Seventeen

Present Day

Margorie was still awake when the message dinged on her phone. She rolled over in bed, feeling half in a dream, and peered down at the screen, frowning. It was from Estelle Coleman. Her heart hammered with dread.

Margorie donned her robe and took her computer downstairs, where she brewed a cup of tea and watched snow flutter beyond her window. It was nearly midnight. She felt no closer to sleep than she had last night, when she'd stayed up for hours, wondering if her romance with Daniel was over before it had even properly begun. Now, she realized Estelle was wide awake, too. For whatever reason, this made her feel less alone.

As far as Margorie knew, Estelle still lived on Nantucket, just a hop over the Nantucket Sound from Margorie's beach house on Martha's Vineyard. But Margorie hadn't picked Martha's Vineyard because of its proximity to Estelle Coleman. She hadn't thought of

Estelle Coleman in years. She'd picked the island because her husband, Tom, had always loved it— and because she'd gotten a good deal on this particular beach house, the result of a longstanding business contact of Tom's.

Margorie sipped her tea and watched the time tick slowly toward one in the morning. She wondered what Estelle did with herself when she couldn't sleep. Did she write? Did she journal? Did she wake Roland up and chat with him deep into the night? After all, they were love-birds, up against the world together. Presumably, they never ran out of things to say to one another. Oh, the thought of it made her heart very dark. She hated the word "jealousy." She wanted to believe she was above it. But was anyone?

Margorie remembered when she'd first finished *A Christmas Dream*. It was more than five years ago, the summer before it was set for release, and her editor had called her to say, "That's all I need. The edits are done. Go out and celebrate!"

Margorie called Tom immediately. "Guess what?" she cried. "It's done!"

"You're kidding!" Tom was euphoric. "Babe, I'm over the moon for you. We have to go out for dinner tonight. My treat."

They decided to check out the new Thai restaurant in downtown Wilmington, where a Thai-American man had opened an exclusive kitchen with only four tables in the dining room. Reservations were required. Due to Tom's connections, he was able to nab them a two-seater that night without a problem. Although Margorie would have fallen in love with him even if he didn't have two pennies to rub together, she still appreciated these perks.

Tom planned to head straight from the office to the

restaurant, which gave Margorie plenty of time to play dress-up. She hung out in her underwear, doing her hair and makeup and listening to music. It felt as though she floated on a cloud of happiness. For decades now, she'd enjoyed a gorgeous romance writing career, one beyond her wildest dreams. She was so grateful she'd found a man who wanted to celebrate that – a man who went out of his way to remind her that her professional accomplishments were just as wonderful as his.

Margorie had met Tom during her senior year at the University of Massachusetts. By that time, she'd lost her shyness, bought a few miniskirts, and begun to believe in herself, which was the beginning of a process that would last her entire life. She had two very good girlfriends, both of whom lent her nicer clothes and gave her pep-talks when times were tough. She worked three jobs, took a full course-load, and had scholarships to ensure she didn't go completely hungry— but she was frequently exhausted. Still, she found time to attend off-campus parties and concerts and go on dates here and there. The dates had largely been disastrous, although she'd gotten the hang of kissing, a skill she'd never thought she'd take on. At one of these parties, she'd met Tom, a business student in bell-bottoms with a laugh louder than an oncoming train. She'd fallen for him the minute he'd looked her in the eyes and smiled in that singular way of his. The smile, she'd known immediately, had been meant only for her – and it had told her something: that she and Tom were meant for something beyond her wildest dreams. They'd been married the year after she'd graduated, after which they'd tried and failed to have children for nearly six years. Margorie hadn't minded much when it hadn't worked out. She'd seen what terrible parents she'd had, and she'd privately worried she wouldn't be much better. Tom had been broken-hearted, but he'd worked through it – telling her over and over again that she was all he needed. He was the best man in the world.

Margorie reached the Thai restaurant five minutes early and sat at the wooden table, reading the menu. Tom had a wonderful palate and exquisite taste, and he pushed her to try new culinary things all the time. She was pretty sure neither of her parents had ever even heard of Thailand, let alone tried the country's food, and she tried to imagine what they'd say if they saw her there with Tom. Would they be proud of how far she'd made it in the world? Or would they find a way to belittle her?

Of course: Margorie had learned her parents had died nearly ten years ago. It had frazzled her for half a year, a time she'd weighed up her decision never to reach out to them or to never lend a helping hand. Had they waited for her? Had they assumed she'd eventually forgive them and return?

The waiter arrived and took her drink order, a chardonnay. "My husband will be here soon," she said. "He always tries something new. Otherwise, I would order for him."

"No rush," the waiter assured her. "We have all night."

Margorie sipped her chardonnay and stared out the window, daydreaming about the upcoming Christmas season. With A Christmas Dream coming out, she was bound for a book tour, presumably one that would sweep her across both coasts and through the Midwest. She adored those middle states, Michigan, Ohio, Indiana, and Illinois; she adored the way her readership there asked her over for tea and wine, yearning to draw her deeper into their cozy communities. Although she'd been born on the east coast and planned to live out her life there, she loved finding herself in the midst of these strangers. They felt they knew her, if only because they read her books religiously.

Five minutes late drifted to fifteen, then twenty. Margorie was half-finished with her glass of wine and checking her phone every thirty seconds for news from Tom. He usually wasn't this late. Then again, anything could have happened. Maybe he'd been held up at the office. Maybe he was caught in traffic. Maybe he'd had to pull over to talk to someone on the phone, a friend who needed him. That was so like Tom, always making time for people who asked for it.

But at forty-five minutes without a word from Tom, Margorie grew irritated. The waiter returned to her table with a fresh glass of chardonnay, which she immediately spilled on her lap. "Oh, goodness," she hissed at herself, pressing a napkin onto her thigh. For the fifth time in fifteen minutes, she called Tom's cell, but it rang forever without answer. Maybe Tom had left it at work by accident. That wasn't like him, but people made mistakes. Even her perfect husband.

Margorie would never forget the look on the cop's face as he entered the Thai restaurant. He was pale as a fish, as though no oxygen had ever entered his bloodstream. He removed his hat when he reached Margorie's table and said, "Are you Margorie Tomlinson?" The look in his eyes had told Margorie everything she'd needed to know, but still, she'd refused the truth. He'd told her Tom had been in an accident; he'd told her he'd died at the hospital after the doctors had been unable to revive him. Vitriol had taken over Margorie's tongue, and she'd said,

"Do you even know who I am?" Which was crazy. Why would this police officer know about Margorie, a romance novelist? He didn't look like the type. Instead of arguing with her, the police officer bowed his head and said, "Tom's secretary told us you had dinner plans tonight. That's how we found you." This news had smacked Margorie over the head. She'd had a headache for days.

After Tom's death, Margorie hadn't even bothered to try to write. She'd locked herself away in Wilmington, scarcely emerging and allowing friends to visit infrequently. *A Christmas Dream* was published that winter to middling acclaim and decent book sales, but she hardly paid it any mind. In fact, if she remembered correctly, she'd spent that winter watching *The Price is Right*, *Dancing with the Stars*, and *The Bachelor* with religious fervor, no longer interested in reading. Her editor and agent had begged her to do a few book signings here and there since she wasn't up for a tour, but she refused.

Now, on Martha's Vineyard five years after the publishing of *A Christmas Dream*, Margorie mounted the stairs of her beachside bungalow and retrieved *A Christmas Dream* from the little library nook. She had numerous copies of it on a high shelf, all stacked up next to one another, mostly untouched. She inhaled the smell of unread pages, slats of very thin wood taken from a tree that had grown for no reason but this. It seemed like a waste.

"Tom, what should I do?" Margorie whispered as she flicked through the pages. Her heart thudded. It was a rare thing for her to speak to her husband aloud like this, as though he were just a room away. She half-imagined him lurking on the other side of the library wall, perhaps changing out of his day's outfit and into a pair of pajama pants. There was nothing Tom liked more than being cozy at home.

But it was as though Tom spoke through her. She could feel the vibrations of his voice through her chest, and she closed her eyes, allowing several tears to flicker down her cheek.

To add insult to injury, when she returned downstairs, there was a message from Daniel on her phone.

DANIEL: Hi.

DANIEL: Can we talk?

Margorie immediately turned off her phone. Too many conflicting thoughts circled her mind, drowning her in confusion. Perhaps she would never sleep again.

Chapter Eighteen

Margorie didn't email Estelle back. She didn't even text Daniel. When her lawyer reached out about pushing forward litigation regarding Estelle's plagiarism, she didn't write him, either. She felt like an island far out in the open sea, without any contact with the outside world. For two days, she sat with her sorrow, her shoulders heavy and her mind rushing, skipping through the channels on her television until she gave up and watched reruns of a crime show on a streaming site. Had Tom been around, perhaps they'd have walked the frigid beach hand-in-hand, skipping stones across the frothing water. Had Tom been there, perhaps they'd have cooked together, Margorie slicing and dicing garlic and onion as Tom played T. Rex or David Bowie on his Bluetooth speaker, dancing through the kitchen.

On the third day of her self-imposed prison, Margorie showered, dressed, and drove across the island to Edgartown. Edgartown was the cozy sister town of Oak Bluffs, with the added benefit of being miles away from Daniel's bookstore. Margorie's plan was to roam the streets, drink a cappuccino, and be amongst people who didn't know her. It was her way of returning to real life for a bit.

Edgartown was dressed to the nines with Christmas spirit. Christmas lights were strung overhead, glinting, and a nativity scene was set up near the courthouse featuring Baby Jesus, Mary, and Joseph. Margorie watched as a little girl knelt beside the Baby Jesus and touched his blanket gently, her eyes reverent. Her mother hurried up behind her, nervous that her daughter would mess up the arrangement. Margorie thought of the children Tom had wanted to have with her, how her body had let him down. How she ached.

But when Margorie turned a random corner in Edgartown, she found herself face-to-face with a bookstore window. At the top of the window were the words: "Who Did It Better?" And within the window were numerous copies of only two books: *A Christmas Dream* and *A Bright Christmas*, Estelle's novel. Margorie's stomach curdled. Obviously, her online feud had become a marketing opportunity in every single way. It had grown into a monster, one she'd birthed herself. She'd begun to hate herself for it. There was no escape.

Margorie gaped at the display for a long time, her hands in fists. She was considering bursting through the door and demanding that the books be removed from the window. After all, she was the author; didn't she have some kind of say? But then the bell above the door jangled, and she heard a familiar voice. "Margorie?"

It was Daniel. He stepped out onto the porch of the store, his eyes earnest with disbelief. This was the single-worst possible outcome. Embarrassment shrouded her.

Without thinking twice, Margorie turned on her heel and sped away from the bookstore, ready to burst into a sprint.

"Margorie! Wait!"

Daniel's footfalls were heavy behind her, crunching through the snow of the front yard of the bookstore. Margorie's heartbeat intensified. Still, she couldn't outrun him. He was younger and far more fit; on top of that, Margorie was wearing heeled boots, a foolish move done in the name of fashion. Steeling herself against any emotion, Margorie set her jaw and turned back to glare at him there on the sidewalk. Daniel stopped a few feet away from her, his face marred with pain.

"What is that?" Margorie demanded, pointing at the window display.

Daniel raised his shoulders.

"And what are you doing here?" Margorie demanded, her voice breaking. She hadn't spoken to anyone in many days at that point, and it was as though her voice box had given out on her. It had lost its battery life. It needed to be greased.

Daniel's cheeks were already bright red from the cold. "I told you," he said finally. "I'm friendly with Heidi, the long-time owner of the bookstore. I buy baked goods from Maggie, the other owner."

A memory wiggled in the back of Margorie's mind. Had he told her that? Had they ever been so close, sharing such intimacies?

Daniel took a step toward her. "Heidi doesn't even know you live on the island," he said softly. "She and Maggie put the window display up just a few days ago, thinking it would get people into the store. This 'feud,' or whatever they're calling it, is good for book sales. And you know how difficult it is to own a bookstore in this day and age."

Margorie blinked back tears, trying to tell herself not to care about this. But she was at the edge of her rope.

Daniel took another step toward her. Margorie felt like a wounded animal in the woods.

"Get a cup of coffee with me," Daniel whispered. "Please."

Margorie wanted to retreat. She wanted to tell Daniel she no longer had any time for him, that she'd promised herself she would remain alone for the rest of her days. But the thought of returning to her beachside bungalow to live out the rest of the afternoon and evening alone was a death sentence.

"A quick coffee," she said, her voice cracking. "But after that, I have to go."

Daniel led Margorie around the corner to a sailing-themed coffee shop. There, a barista with a fuzzy white headband made them cappuccinos and gave them a slice of pie to share "on the house." Margorie wanted to tell the barista they were the last people on earth who wanted pie right now, up until Daniel struck the pie with a fork, took a bite, and smiled. "It's divine," he told her. "Margorie, you have to try it." The look in his eyes meant business.

Margorie spooned herself a heap of the apple-cinnamon pie and closed her eyes. The crust was crisp and gooey at once, and the apples were tart yet seemed to melt in her mouth as though they were made of caramel. When her eyes flickered back open, Daniel was smiling at her gently, his eyes still lit with whatever hope he'd had for them before the Christmas party at the Aquinnah Cliffside Overlook Hotel.

Margorie set down the fork quietly and laced her

fingers together on her lap. What did Daniel want her to say? Did he want her to explain more about the feud? Did he want her to draw him a general map of why she was filled with such despair, to explain why her heart was quite this broken?

"I'm sorry everything got so mixed up the other night at the party," Daniel said finally, breaking through her anxious thoughts.

Margorie shook her head. Her head throbbed as she searched for the right thing to say.

"I don't think Kelli was trying to be mean," Daniel went on. "She's a curious person by nature. But I'm sorry it came out the way it did. No wonder you wanted to get away from me the first chance you could."

Margorie's heart dropped into her stomach. "That wasn't it," Margorie whispered, surprising herself.

Daniel tilted his head and gave her a look of incredulity.

Margorie stared beyond Daniel's head toward a painting of a lighthouse near the corner. She couldn't look him in the eye as she said, "The thing is, I've never even read Estelle's new book." Her voice shattered at the edges. "When I read about its themes and its characters in the blurb, I jumped to a horrible conclusion. Somewhere in the back of my very dark and lonely mind, I decided to take Estelle down with me." Margorie rubbed her temples and closed her eyes. "I don't think I fully knew I was doing it at the time, but I see it more and more clearly now. And I feel like a monster."

Now that she'd said it aloud, a weight shifted from her shoulders. For the first time in many days, Margorie took a full, deep breath. Daniel reached across the table to touch her hand, and his touch felt too intense. Margorie moved her hand to the side as her eyes smarted.

"Margorie," Daniel began, sounding hesitant. "Whatever happened, it can be fixed."

"I don't know. I think it's too late."

Daniel rubbed his chin with the back of his hand. "Sometimes, when we're deeply in pain, it can be easy to lose context. Help me understand everything. Please. I promise I'll help you through."

Chapter Nineteen

1971

During the week after Thanksgiving, Estelle forced her life into a different rhythm. Now that she and Roland were officially over, now that she'd thrust him as far away from her, emotionally, as she could, she needed to find a different thing to live for. Maybe, armed with the *How to Write a Novel* book, she could make writing her identity. Maybe she could even get half-good if she worked hard enough. And Estelle wasn't the sort of young woman to shy away from hard work. The past six months of back-breaking work, alienation from her father and boyfriend, and nursing her mother through her cancer was proof of that.

Every night after her mother fell asleep, Estelle sat at the kitchen table with a very small glass of red wine, a bowl of nuts, her notebook, and her writing guide. At first, she did the writing exercises outlined in the book, prompts that demanded: "describe the room you're sitting in," or "write a character profile for your father," or "write out an action scene at your high school." These stretched her vocabulary and forced her to regain familiarity with her inner voice. But after a week of that, Estelle grew tired of the basics. Perhaps because he'd possessed her in some way, Estelle decided to write about Roland, about the love they'd shared. Maybe, in writing about it, she would find a way to remove all thoughts of Roland from her mind. Maybe she could start over.

Initially, Estelle considered starting from the beginning. But when was the beginning, exactly? Being islanders, Estelle and Roland had known one another since they were four years old. They'd attended the same preschool, probably stacking blocks side-by-side with drool and crumbs down their cheeks.

Estelle had first considered Roland to be "cute," her word, around the age of eleven. Girls traditionally thought about boys earlier than boys thought about girls, which was a curse that lingered with them throughout their lifetimes. Estelle laughed when she remembered she'd had a crush on someone else first, a shaggy-haired blonde boy who'd drawn pictures throughout class. What had been his name? Jared? Ultimately, he'd moved away, and Estelle's eyes had settled on Roland Coleman. A shiver raced up her spine. She started to write.

Estelle wrote about her and Roland's middle school and high school romance, about the school dances they'd attended and the kisses they'd shared. She wrote all the way up to the summer of 1971, at which point the story deviated. In this version, she and Roland actually made it to the University of Massachusetts, where they ate at that pizza place down the street from their apartment, helped each other study, made heaps of friends, and graduated at the top of their class. By the time she graduated, she was pregnant with their first child, a fact they hid from their families before they were married three months later. Afterward, they moved so that Roland could attend MIT and Estelle could attend Harvard, where they, miraculously, were able to raise their baby and become world-renowned intellectuals.

Estelle knew it was partially insane to write this out. It was like punching herself in the heart over and over again, a continual reminder of just how sad she was about all she'd lost. But as she poured herself out over the page, she grew increasingly enamored with the creative process. By the first week of December, she'd already read through the *How to Write a Novel* book one and a half times. A strange thought struck her: she was only at the beginning of her writing career. She'd only just begun.

Even if she never got married, even if she never had a baby, even if she never left Nantucket – she would always be a writer. She knew that in her soul.

Estelle finally felt confident enough in her writing to confess to Jessabelle. "I've written almost an entire book," she said sheepishly, hovering at a library shelf with a book raised.

Jessabelle's eyes widened. "And? How is it?"

"I'm sure it's terrible," Estelle said, blushing. "I'm sure I made one thousand mistakes. But it's the best feeling I've had in months."

Jessabelle squeezed her elbow gently. "I'm so proud of you. I can't wait to read your first book when it's published! I hope I'll get a signed copy."

"That's a long way from now," Estelle assured her with a laugh. "I'm just a novice."

"Everyone starts somewhere," Jessabelle reminded her. "Just keep going."

During the second week of December, Estelle braved the sharp Nantucket cold and drove out to the Christmas tree farm. Traditionally, her mother and father had always selected the tree together, alternating between fighting about how to decorate it and complimenting its beauty. Normally, those nights had ended with her father too drunk to get off the couch and her mother sighing by the tree, captivated with her life after one too many glasses of white wine. It had always mystified Estelle. Now that her father was long gone and her mother was still weak from her previous round of treatments, Estelle felt the weight of Christmas tradition upon her shoulders. She had no plans to ignore the holiday, but she had to do it in a way that didn't remind her mother of everything she'd lost.

Estelle picked out a medium-sized Christmas tree with a full body and a pointed top. An employee at the farm helped her tie the tree to the top of her car and took her money— just two dollars. When Estelle returned home that night, her heart pumped with expectation. She couldn't wait to decorate it and surprise her mother when she woke up tomorrow.

Estelle stayed up till past midnight, drawing garlands and lights around the tree, filling the base with water, and hanging bulbs that, she hoped, had nothing to do with her mother's memories with her father. As she scrambled up onto a chair to place the angel at the top, there was a creak from the hallway that frightened her, and she nearly tumbled to the ground.

"Honey. What is this?" Carrie's voice was groggy and filled with sleep.

Estelle turned to see her leaning against the doorway in her white nightgown. She looked like a ghost, her long, thin face drawn, and a thick knitted hat pulled over her ears. It was impossible to believe that Carrie had ever had a lush, healthy-looking head of hair. Estelle remembered being a child, seated on her mother and father's bed, watching as her mother swept her brush through her locks.

Carrie limped into the living room and collapsed on the couch, her eyes gleaming with the light of the tree. For a moment, Estelle was terrified she'd yell at her, that she'd say Estelle's decorating made her even more miserable. But then, her mother's eyes filled with tears.

"It's stunning, darling." Carrie pressed her hands over her face, and her shoulders sagged forward. "I don't even know what to say."

Estelle sat next to her mother and touched her shoulder. All she wanted was to take her mother's pain away. All she wanted was for things to go back to how they'd been. But it was impossible.

"I know this year has been tough on you," Carrie said, shifting toward Estelle to lay her head on her shoulder.

"I'm not the one who's sick," Estelle reminded her quietly.

"No. But you're the one who's had to carry me through this. You're the one who's worked so many hours at that terrible restaurant, who's shelved thousands upon thousands of books." Carrie was quiet. "You're the one who put off your studying plans to support me here."

Estelle shivered. A part of her had thought her mother had been too out of it, too tired, too sick to even notice what Estelle was doing.

"It was all that mattered to me," Estelle whispered. "It was all I really wanted to do."

Carrie patted her hand. For a little while, they sat in silence, enthralled by the tree.

And then, her mother asked: "Have you seen Roland since he left for college?"

Estelle's heartbeat quickened. Her mother hadn't brought up Roland's name once since August. "I haven't seen him, no."

"Do you think you'll see him when he comes home for Christmas?"

"No. I don't." Estelle swallowed. "I think it's healthier for me not to see him."

Carrie sighed. "You're smarter than I was at your age."

"I don't think that's true." Estelle didn't feel very smart at all just then. She felt useless, tired, too thin, the jagged edge of something broken.

"Do you still want the things you used to want?" Carrie asked. "Do you still want to get married and have a family?"

"Of course," Estelle said. "I've always wanted that. And so much more."

Carrie nodded.

"And I'm coming around to the idea that I can do those things without Roland," Estelle said. "I heard a rumor there are other men on the island. Smart, handsome men."

"Is that so?"

Estelle chuckled despite the ache in her heart. It had been ages since her mother had made a joke. "Maybe in a year or two, I'll be able to go out on another date again. I don't know. It's hard to imagine myself out with anyone else. But the only constant thing in life is change, right?

And I'll find a way to be ready for that next chapter. Somehow."

Carrie squeezed her hand. "Let me know if I can support you, honey. I want to be there for you the way you've been here for me."

That night, Estelle stayed up much later than she'd planned for, writing and editing what she called the "What Should Have Been" book. At three-thirty, she collapsed in bed and slept a dreamless sleep until she awoke at the first light of morning, ready to start the workday all over again. She was in the endless slog of life — and she had to find a way to brew magic within it. It would be an endless struggle.

But that night, after Estelle returned home from work, she was hit with a tremendous surprise.

Her mother was asleep in bed, shrouded in darkness. Estelle took this opportunity to head to her room and continue to write her book. But when she reached her desk, she found her notebook wasn't where she'd left it. She flung open the desk's drawers, hunted beneath the bed, and scoured her bookshelf. Her heartbeat was so loud she thought it would shatter her eardrums.

Panicked, Estelle ran into the kitchen, just in case she'd left the notebook on the counter by accident. Sure enough, it sat on the counter. But there was something off about it.

Estelle realized what was wrong a split second later. Most of the pages had been torn out of the center of the notebook, leaving behind jagged spits of paper.

The new first page of the notebook had upon it the following message, written in pen:

My darling Estelle,

I found this notebook on your desk. I cried from the

first page to the very last. You are a gorgeous writer – the most talented I've ever read. (I'm biased, of course, but I simply had no idea how remarkable you were. And I'm your mother!)

Perhaps because I'm sick and sad and very strange right now, I immediately tore out the pages, put them in an envelope, and mailed them off to the University of Massachusetts. Roland needs to see them.

Before you get cross with me, remember that I was once a young woman in love, too. When I fell in love with your father, I was out of my mind with thoughts of him. I followed him around like a lost puppy and eventually ended up in a sad, alcohol-fueled marriage and subsequent divorce. But Roland is not like your father. And you are not like me. You have done everything you can to be completely independent. And if that independence truly separates you and Roland from one another forever, so be it.

But I have a hunch Roland isn't over you. And I see from these pages that you won't be over Roland any time soon. He has to know how much you love him, honey. He has to see.

Love, Mom

Chapter Twenty

"I don't know how to explain myself," Margorie said softly, her eyes on the dark liquid in her coffee mug. She was seated at the coffee shop with Daniel across from her, his eyes big, glinting pools she wanted to fall into. He'd told her he was a good listener, that he would help her through this horrific time if she let him. He just wanted her to let him in. She wasn't sure why he wanted to be so nice to her. Did he think he was going to get something out of it?

"Just start from the beginning," Daniel offered. "I don't have any plans."

Margorie emptied her coffee mug and rubbed her thighs, her eyes flickering around the coffee shop. Outside, a cerulean sky arched over snow-capped Edgartown, and she had the sudden desire to be out in it, marching through the streets to match the intensity of her swirling thoughts.

"Do you mind if we go for a walk?"

Daniel paid for their coffees and opened the door for her, following her into the blistering cold. Out there, her thoughts crystallized, and she was able to breathe deeper.

"I'm sorry," Margorie said after a moment. "It was so hot in that coffee shop. I thought I was going to faint."

"It's okay," Daniel assured her. "We can run all over the island, as far as I'm concerned. And it's a gorgeous day. I feel like I haven't seen the sun in weeks."

Margorie stopped on the sidewalk and glared at him, searching his face for some sign that he was making fun of her. Had Kelli sent him to poke and prod her for information about the feud with Estelle Coleman? Was he a secret agent doing her dirty work?

They walked quietly for a while. Margorie realized she was headed eastward toward the harbor, where the lighthouse towered over the port proudly despite its lack of use in the previous decades. Margorie made a mental note to read more about the history of Martha's Vineyard; had Tom been there, he probably could have told her when that lighthouse had been built, who had designed it, and how many whaling ships had left from that harbor four hundred years ago.

"Do you know when that lighthouse was built?" Margorie asked Daniel spontaneously.

Daniel scratched his forehead under his winter hat. "1828," he said with a smile. "If I remember correctly. Martha's Vineyard history was drilled into us in high school. Why do you ask?"

"I was just curious," Margorie breathed. "It's been a while since I learned anything new."

"I understand that. It's easy to fall into ruts, isn't it?" Daniel's smile was sorrowful. "Right now, I feel like I'm in the midst of a personal re-evaluation. I just got divorced, and I'm asking myself questions about who I want to be next and what my morals are."

Margorie swallowed. So lost in her own pitfalls, she'd hardly stopped to consider Daniel's only assessment of himself. She felt terribly selfish. She leaned over the railing and gazed up at the lighthouse, listening to the caw of seagulls overhead. And then she said: "Since my husband died, I haven't felt like myself. Or, to put it another way, I've felt exactly the way I used to feel as a younger woman."

"Regression?" Daniel suggested. "I understand that. I've felt that way so much since my ex-wife left the island. I'm constantly battling my own thought processes, reminding myself of all I've learned over the years. Of how far I've come."

Margorie locked eyes with him for a moment and nodded. "Yes. Exactly that. It's bizarre to have the body of an older woman while I'm thinking the thoughts of a much lonelier, nervous younger woman." Her heart thudded as she demanded herself to tell him more. Maybe Daniel deserved it. Maybe he was worthy of her trust.

"Back when I was eighteen, I left my abusive father and a mother who didn't care so much for me and went to the University of Massachusetts on a full scholarship. My family couldn't understand why I wanted to go to school at all. They saw it as a waste of time. My father, especially, said I thought I was better than all of them. He was an alcoholic in the purest sense of the word. But back then, it was a little more common, a little more expected. Even when he hit me, I thought I deserved it."

Daniel's eyes widened with surprise, but he didn't speak.

"When I went to college, I struggled to make friends,"

Margorie went on, her voice catching. "I had been a huge loner in high school, obviously, and in college, I felt my father's voice echoing in my head, reminding me that I wasn't good enough. It was debilitating. But in my literature class, I had a huge crush on this very handsome guy."

Daniel's smile was soft and sincere. He looked as though he genuinely wanted to hear what Margorie had to say.

"His name was Roland," Margorie went on, "and he was so intelligent and earnest. We started spending more and more time together. I made up a fantasy in my head that we were going to run away together and write books side-by-side. When I had to go home for Thanksgiving break, I told my family I had a boyfriend, even though we'd never even kissed before.

"But on the night of Thanksgiving, my father got drunk and almost hit me. I couldn't believe it. I thought I'd grown beyond that abuse. Immediately, I called Roland, and he drove all the way from Nantucket to my hometown to save me. We spent that night in a hotel, talking for hours. I'd never felt closer to another person in my life.

"We went back to the University of Massachusetts the next day, and I spent the weekend at his apartment until I was allowed to return to my dormitory," Margorie went on. "Nothing romantic ever happened, but we made pancakes and played records and talked about everything. I thought if I just waited around a little bit more and played it cool, he would eventually figure out that we were perfect for one another." Margorie laughed gently at herself.

"Maybe two or three weeks later, everyone at the University of Massachusetts was drowning in preparation for finals," Margorie remembered. "I didn't hear from Roland as often, and I didn't run into him anymore because classes were finished to make time for studying and exams. Finally, I walked off campus to his apartment and knocked on the door. Stupidly, I'd bought him a box of Christmas chocolates, thinking we could eat and complain about finals. But when Roland opened the door, the look on his face told me everything had changed."

Daniel grimaced.

"His apartment was in a state of chaos," Margorie went on, remembering the scene. "He'd removed every article of clothing from his closet and thrown it into suitcases. He was manic, saying he had to go back to Nantucket the very next day. I asked him about finals. Didn't we have our literature final in three days' time? But he said he had no plans to wait around. He said he didn't care about school anymore. I was flabbergasted. Eventually, he sat at the edge of his bed, which was stripped of bedding, and showed me a stack of pages that had been torn out of a notebook. He explained that his girlfriend had written a book about their love and that he wanted to go back to Nantucket and make her dream come true. This was staggering to hear. I'd thought Roland and I were building our own romance story! But the look in his eyes told me he was really and truly in love with her. Whatever I'd thought we had, it was over.

"I was broken-hearted, of course. In one fell swoop, I'd lost my love and my best friend. He never returned to campus after that. He never even wrote me a letter! Oh, but I never could have imagined that that ex-girlfriend, his wife, would become another top-selling romance novelist. When I first met her at a romance convention maybe twenty years ago, I was so stricken that I had to take a moment in the bathroom to patch myself back up. By then, I was head-over-heels in love with my husband, Tom, and I had no real qualms about Roland and I not working out. But even still, it felt so bizarre to meet her in the flesh. Estelle Coleman! Coleman, the last name I'd wanted for myself!

"But since Tom died," Margorie went on, "I haven't been as kind as I want to be. I haven't been myself. And when I saw that Estelle's newest book, *A Bright Christmas*, centered around themes of *A Christmas Dream*, something in my mind broke down. I was so jealous of the life she'd been allowed to have with Roland, a life I felt I should have had instead. I started making accusations. I started screaming at the abyss of the internet. And now, I'm too far gone."

Margorie pressed her hands over her face and exhaled all the air from her lungs. The tremendous weight of the story made the air around them heavier. Suddenly, Daniel touched her shoulder, reminding her she wasn't alone.

"You must think I'm so evil," Margorie whispered.

"What?" Daniel laughed kindly. "No. I could never think you're evil."

Margorie turned to face him again. "I hate that I did this to her."

"You can take it back," Daniel breathed. "And you can start writing again. People adore your books, you know. They just want more stories from that amazing brain of yours." He paused before adding, "I've already read two of your books since I met you. And I'm craving more."

Margorie's lips parted with surprise. "You read my novels?"

Daniel's laugh echoed across the harbor. "How could

I resist? I've been fascinated with you since I met you. All of your books tugged at my heartstrings." He pressed his lips together. "They made me fall for you even more. It's been dangerous yet so beautiful."

Margorie was genuinely at a loss for words. For a long time, she gazed into Daniel's eyes, daring herself to wake up from this dream. Had she really just confessed the innermost darkness of her heart, only to be accepted? Wasn't it too good to be true?

Chapter Twenty One

On Wednesday morning, Estelle awoke before dawn. Outside the window was the yawn of a gray morning, light dripping across the waves. She brewed a pot of coffee and stretched out her aching limbs, her head pounding. Her phone said many things, mostly regarding the numerous fans reaching out to her after the video she'd posted with Rachelle and Darcy. She couldn't help but feel foolish about that. She wasn't a teenager.

With a mug of coffee in hand, Estelle checked her email, expecting nothing. Ever since the publisher had dropped her series, her agent, Christie, had checked in less and less, making Estelle feel very alone in her silly writing feud.

But that's when she realized it. Margorie had responded to her message.

Estelle.

Thanks for reaching out. I'm currently living in a beach house on Martha's Vineyard.

Would you like to come to my place this week?
Maybe we can have a chat.

Best, Margorie.

Estelle's heart hammered in her chest. She darkened her phone and hurried into her office, where she sat at the edge of her desk chair and considered what to do. All this time, Margorie had been one island away from her. All this time, she'd been spitting vitriol about Estelle's career from literally only miles away. Estelle didn't know what to make of it. She tried to imagine what it would be like to go to Martha's Vineyard to visit her, but her mind was blank. In what world would she sit with Margorie Tomlinson and actually speak rationally? Hadn't they already been through too much?

Estelle wasn't able to write at all that morning. By lunchtime, she was anxious and jittery, considering throwing herself into a household task, even one she hated, in order to get her mind off of things. She paraded through the kitchen, slicing and dicing vegetables for a salad, as Roland smeared mayonnaise across a piece of bread and frowned.

"What's going on, honey?"

Estelle grimaced and glared at him. She wanted to tell him he couldn't possibly understand.

"I finally heard from Margorie Tomlinson about our feud," she said.

Roland's face was slack and suddenly very pale.

"She wants me to come to Martha's Vineyard to talk," Estelle stammered. "But I feel like it's a trap. She hasn't shown me any goodwill from the start. Why should I trust her now?"

Roland set his knife back onto the plate before him and wiped away nothing on his thighs. For a little while, he stared somewhere above Estelle's head as though he couldn't fully face her, which made her feel outside of herself. And then, he spoke.

"I finally put together the connection," he said, "about how I know Margorie Tomlinson."

Estelle's jaw dropped with surprise. Was she dreaming?

"We went to the University of Massachusetts together," Roland explained.

"What?" Estelle shook her head, flabbergasted. She remembered Roland, returning to Nantucket after only a semester away, too thin, his eyes earnest. She'd hardly allowed herself to imagine the life he'd had so far from home. It had hurt too much to think about the world he'd attempted to build for himself. And besides— it hadn't been enough for him. He'd jumped at the chance to return.

"She was in my literature class," Roland explained. "She was very smart, and we hung out a little bit. I think she was the loneliest person I'd ever met." Roland rubbed his eyes, looking exhausted. "Her father was abusive toward her. On Thanksgiving night, she called up my parents' house and told me he'd almost hit her. I got in the car and went to the ferry immediately."

Estelle's heart hammered with shock. She remembered Thanksgiving that year, how Roland had come to her door begging her to answer it. She hadn't. And he'd gone elsewhere.

"Nothing ever happened between us," Roland said into his hands. "I know she wanted it to. I know she had a big crush on me. But that was so many years ago, Estelle. I never imagined she'd pop back into our world like this."

"And nearly destroy my career," Estelle whispered.

Roland rolled his shoulders back and gave her a pointed look. "If she wants to talk this out, it means she knows what she's done. I didn't know Margorie for very long, but I know her enough to say this. She feels like a fool for having started this. Let her explain."

"You don't know her," Estelle protested. "You were friendly with her, briefly, fifty years ago."

"People don't change that much," Roland offered. "We haven't. Have we?"

Estelle leaned against the counter and watched the snow flutter out the window. Just a few miles across the Nantucket Sound, across the rolling hills of Martha's Vineyard, tucked away on a beach somewhere, Margorie sat, awaiting her answer. If she'd been a smarter woman, Estelle wouldn't have even considered going over there. She would have kept her head down, continued talking to her fans via TikTok, and plotted out her next novel.

But something in Roland's eyes told her this was important. Maybe her and Margorie's stories had always been inextricably linked, and Estelle had just never been the wiser.

Chapter Twenty Two

Estelle drove alone to the ferry and parked deep within the vessel. Very few people parked alongside her. It was only a few days till Christmas, and nobody had any need to go anywhere or do anything that wasn't cozy and surrounded by family at home. Estelle jumped out and walked up to the coffee shop, where she purchased a black coffee in a paper cup and stood by the window to watch the Nantucket Sound surge past, gray and formidable. She was terrified of what awaited her on the other side of this trip, terrified that Margorie would say something cutting about her writing or her creativity or her place in life that would make her feel very small.

"Merry Christmas!" the worker at the kiosk told her as he cleaned the countertop and smiled. He wore a Santa hat, and it bobbed around as he cleaned.

"And to you," Estelle said. "Do you have plans for the holidays?"

"I'll be on this ferry," he said with a laugh that showed a few missing teeth. "My family is long gone, and they need someone to work. But I don't mind. I love the open sea."

Estelle's heart cracked at the edges. Yet, as she searched the man's face for signs of sorrow, she found none. To him, the "open sea" was the same route, from Martha's Vineyard to Nantucket and back again, over and over again. Yet he found a way to delight in it. There was a lesson in there somewhere, Estelle knew.

When the ferry docked in Martha's Vineyard, Estelle cranked her engine and rolled easily from the ferry, dropping her wheels back on solid ground. Margorie had sent her beach house address, which Estelle pulled up on her phone's GPS. It was fifteen minutes away.

As Estelle drove, she remembered something— the horrific day when Roland had come to Martha's Vineyard by chance and discovered his father, Chuck Coleman, eating at a restaurant with his second family. Neither of them had been able to believe it. Estelle had watched her father storm out the door and never speak to her or her mother again. But Chuck Coleman had seemed too good for something like that. He'd seemed like a genuine family man.

What was it about Martha's Vineyard? It felt like the sister island to Nantucket in some ways, but it was also indecipherable for Estelle. And now, it just so happened to host Margorie Tomlinson, the closest thing Estelle had to an enemy.

Margorie's beach house was tucked under a sprawl of oak, maple, and willow trees, its face out toward the frothing Vineyard Sound. Estelle parked in the driveway and watched the doors and windows for some sign of movement. Perhaps this was a trap.

But a split-second later, the door facing the driveway

burst open, and Margorie Tomlinson appeared. She waved a long arm out, beckoning for Estelle to come up, and Estelle jumped out of the car, holding her breath as she crunched through the snow. When she reached the porch, she took in Margorie's features— her soft skin that seemed several decades too young for her, her mermaid red hair, her long limbs that flowed like water as she pushed the door open wider so Estelle could enter. Estelle tried to imagine this woman as the eighteen-year-old who'd been so in love with Roland. Just barely, she could find that youthful face.

"Hi." Estelle's voice was very quiet, and steam spilled from her mouth and into the frigid air on the porch.

"Hi." Margorie tilted her head and peered at Estelle curiously. "I have a fire going."

Without speaking, Estelle followed Margorie into the foyer, where she removed her snow boots, coat, hat, and gloves. Margorie's beach house was decorated similarly to other beach houses— without any real regard for the current guest's personality. Margorie, reading Estelle's mind, said, "I know. There are a lot of lighthouse and seashell paintings around here. If I stay through next year, I'll have it redecorated to suit my taste. Whatever that taste turns out to be." She smiled.

Margorie's joke shot through Estelle, and she bucked with spontaneous laughter. Her shoulders and chest loosened. She hadn't realized how tense she'd been.

Margorie tugged at her long hair nervously. "Would you like a glass of something? I have hot wine. Or cold wine. Or tea."

"Tea sounds nice for now," Estelle said. "Thanks."

Estelle sat on the couch near the fire and warmed her hands as Margorie clattered around the adjoining kitchen, making tea. In the living room were piles upon piles of romance novels, several of which had been written by people Estelle was friendly with. One of them, she saw now, was her book, *A Bright Christmas*. It had a bookmark in it. Was Margorie actually reading it?

A moment later came Estelle's answer. Margorie set the mugs of tea on the coffee table, pressed her hands on her thighs, and nodded toward Estelle's book. "I finally started reading your book."

Estelle's throat was very tight. She prayed she wasn't saying the wrong thing when she asked, "Are you liking it so far?"

Margorie sat on the opposite end of the couch and stared into the fire. Her eyes glinted. "I love your writing, Estelle."

Estelle was speechless yet again. She remained frozen.

"I've always loved it," Margorie went on. "I bought your first book when it came out, and I devoured it in one day. You have such a way with words, with descriptions, and with characters. It's like you fully embody the people in your books if that makes sense. They feel as real as any person I've ever met in real life."

Estelle's cheeks burned at the onslaught of compliments. "I've felt the same way about your books over the years. That one you wrote that was set in Paris?"

"*The Paris Waitress*," Margorie affirmed.

"Yes. I still think about the main character. Her name was Sarah, right? I always think about how she took her coffee with all that cream and no sugar. And that first kiss she shares with Walter! My gosh." Estelle pressed her hand over her heart, genuinely on the verge of tears. "I spent the entire day swooning after I first read that."

Margorie dropped her chin. "I remember writing that kiss," she said after a pause. "I based it off of my first kiss with my husband, Tom. I find it wild that I'm still able to remember the kiss so intimately, even this many years afterward."

"Memory is a funny thing," Estelle agreed.

"Very powerful," Margorie said.

They held the silence for a moment. Estelle finally took her mug of tea and sipped it.

Finally, Margorie said, "I called my lawyer this morning. We've dropped the charges."

Estelle raised her eyebrows and set her tea back down again. "Margorie, I can't even begin to tell you how thankful I am."

Margorie waved both of her hands, palms toward Estelle. Stuttering, she said, "You can't imagine how embarrassed I feel. When I finally sat down with your book, I recognized it for what it really is— a work of fiction that is entirely your own." Margorie raised her shoulders. "I have no real excuse for my behavior the past few weeks. All I can say, I suppose, is that I've been a real mess since my husband died five years ago. I've fallen back into old habits. I've become a sort of monster."

Estelle shook her head, her hair flashing across her shoulders. "You're not a monster. This business is cutthroat. It's gone to my head more times than I can count. I haven't fully recognized myself. And just the other day, my granddaughters helped me make a TikTok video. That isn't me!" Estelle tried to laugh, but it soon faded to leave only the sound of the crackling fire.

Margorie heaved a sigh and forced her eyes back toward Estelle's. She was quiet yet giving Estelle her full attention.

And then, Estelle said, "Why didn't you tell me you knew my husband?"

Margorie didn't look surprised Estelle had brought this up, but she did look very tired.

"I don't know. I suppose when we first met years ago at that romance writing convention, I was too embarrassed to admit it. I had built this big writing career. I didn't want to call attention to the fact that I'd once been left behind at college by my big college crush." There was a soft joke in her voice.

"That must have felt horrible," Estelle offered.

"It did." Margorie laughed gently. "I was such a lonely girl. I built my world around Roland, stupidly. And then, one day, he was gone."

Estelle wanted to tell Margorie how much she related to that. But, she reminded herself, she'd been the one to break up with Roland back in the summer of 1971. She'd pushed him out of her life. She'd forced him to abandon her, in a way.

"I have something to show you," Margorie said, her face suddenly stormy. "But you have to promise not to get angry."

Estelle promised, and Margorie got to her feet and retrieved a folder in the corner of the room, which was balanced upon a tall stack of romance novels. Without opening it, she handed the folder to Estelle and crossed her arms over her chest.

"What is this?" Estelle asked, arching her brow.

Margorie rubbed the back of her neck as Estelle opened the folder and peered down at the first page.

Aloud, she read, "What Should Have Been." And then, she couldn't breathe. Impossibly, the handwriting was her own, yet more youthful, with loops to beautify the scrawl. The writing was similarly childish, showing the skill of a very young writer with big dreams. It was like looking at a time capsule.

Estelle blinked up at Margorie, suddenly petrified. Margorie was shaking.

"Why do you have this?" Estelle rasped.

Margorie raised her shoulders. In a very low voice, she said, "When I went to see Roland before he left, I saw it on his desk. I knew it was the reason he was going back to you; I knew it had tremendous power over him. I suppose I thought if I took it, he would slowly forget why he was leaving college. Maybe he would come back for the second semester." Margorie chuckled. "I was a fool."

Estelle clutched the folder of pages from 1971 to her chest as tears sprung to her eyes. All she could think about right now was her mother's letter, in which she'd admitted she'd sent the manuscript off to Roland at the University of Massachusetts. In that single act, her mother changed the course of Estelle's life forever. When Roland had appeared on her doorstep with a bouquet of roses and the promise never to leave her behind again, Estelle hadn't even thought to ask about the manuscript. She'd had Roland back. She hadn't needed anything else.

"My mother sent these pages to Roland," Estelle whispered. "I can hardly believe they still exist."

"I couldn't believe I still had them," Margorie admitted. "I found them in a box of old things from college a few years ago when I was cleaning out my house after Tom died. I hadn't thought about that time of my life in years. Yet here it was— calling back to me."

Estelle continued to clutch the manuscript as Margorie sat back on the opposite side of the couch. The air had shifted. Estelle felt very intimate with this woman simply because she'd read the very first book she'd ever written. It had been her first attempt, and she'd thrown her entire heart and soul into it.

"I'll make a statement online," Margorie went on, watching the fire. "I'll have my agent send a press release to every major publication to ensure your name is cleared. I'll probably lose thousands of fans. But that's the price of what I've done."

"Just tell them you made a mistake," Estelle breathed. "That's the truth, anyway."

Margorie sighed. "I tried to destroy your career, Estelle. I can't even believe it when I say it aloud. Throughout my time as a romance novelist, I've done my best to build up the careers of the women in my life, not destroy them." Margorie took a long sip of tea, and the cup shook in her hands.

Estelle's heart broke at the sight of this woman. She had the urge to drop down beside her on the couch and wrap her arms around her the way she might have comforted Sam or Hilary long ago.

"Your mother was very sick when you wrote that first manuscript, correct?" Margorie asked. "It's the time you based *A Bright Christmas* on?"

"Yes."

"Did she get well again?"

Estelle's vision shimmered with tears. "She did, for a while. By that next summer, she was athletic and confident again. She'd grown back her hair. It was remarkable to see. Together, we planned my wedding to Roland, and she walked me down the aisle. She was there for all the births of my children, holding my hand."

Margorie stared at Estelle, rapt with attention.

"When my youngest, Hilary, was four, we got the

news that Mom had cancer again," Estelle offered. "It was everywhere this time. I told my mother we would fight together, just as we had last time. But it was too late. She died five months after that last diagnosis. And I think a piece of me died with her."

Estelle's voice cracked as she told the story. Just when she thought she would break down again, Margorie stood and walked over to her side of the couch and sat down beside her. Warmth emanated from her.

"She sounds like an extraordinary woman," Margorie said.

"She really was," Estelle offered. "She's part of the reason I wanted to write *A Bright Christmas* in the first place. I wanted to honor her memory."

"And you did," Margorie whispered. "I can feel how much you love her in your writing. All your readers can, too."

For a little while, Estelle and Margorie watched the fire quietly, neither daring to destroy the comfortable silence they'd finally drawn between them. Outside, afternoon had darkened into early evening. Margorie popped up to turn the lights on her Christmas tree. At the window, she gestured toward the brewing clouds. "You're welcome to stay the night. I heard we're supposed to get some snow."

Estelle found herself chatting with Margorie deep into the night. Margorie got up frequently to place additional logs on the fire or poke the embers before turning back and adding to their conversation, adding density to their very strange and brief friendship. She asked questions about Estelle's previous novels, about Estelle's work on various podcasts, and about Roland, wondering if he'd changed very much in the previous fifty years and if his career had taken off in the way he'd hoped. With each question and fresh conversation, it was as though they saw one another with more clarity. They were both romance novelists getting up there in years, with the majority of their writing careers behind them. It shouldn't have been such a surprise that they got along so well. But it was a marvelous treat to find one another like this in an at-times strange and lonely world. Estelle counted her blessings.

Chapter Twenty-Three

On the afternoon of Christmas Eve, Margorie told Daniel everything she could remember about Estelle's visit. They were seated at a cozy wine bar just a block away from the White Whale Bookstore, Margorie with a glass of Primitivo and Daniel with a Malbec, and a Christmassy snowfall added another inch to the six that already blanketed the rolling hills of Martha's Vineyard.

"I can't believe she actually came over!" Daniel shook his head.

"Me neither. I definitely didn't deserve it," Margorie said quietly.

Daniel placed his hand over hers and gazed into her eyes. "You do deserve it. You're a remarkable woman, Margorie."

"But I made a horrible mistake."

"Do you want to know how many mistakes I made just today?" Daniel asked. "Should I list them out for you?"

Margorie quivered with laughter. "I'm sure you did everything right!"

"All right. Here it goes. First, I gave my grandson the wrong oatmeal," Daniel said, raising his first finger to count. "And then, after he cried and I tried to console him, my mother started to eat the oatmeal and got angry at me because it was already cold. After that, there was a wild knocking at the door, and I realized I'd accidentally locked the front door after my daughter and son-in-law had left for a run."

"None of these are that bad!" Margorie cried.

"Afterwards, I spilled an entire glass of orange juice across the counter," Daniel continued. "And then, while I was shaving in preparation to come meet you, I took a huge chunk out of my beard. Look." Daniel turned his head to show the soft knick along his jawbone.

"And that's all pretty typical stuff," Daniel continued. "If I gave you a list of my actual mistakes, it'd be a mile long."

Margorie sighed and laced her fingers through his across the table. She wanted to ask him why he was too good to be true; she wanted to ask him why he even bothered to make her laugh. But she also didn't want to chase him away with her insecurities. Not again.

"I can't thank you enough," Margorie said quietly.

"For what? For spilling orange juice?"

Margorie quivered with laughter. "No. For being you, I guess. Aren't I the cheesiest person in the world?"

"Lucky for you, I love cheese." Daniel shifted forward on his chair, closed his eyes, and kissed her gently on the lips. Margorie felt as though her soul was floating from her body. When he pulled back very quietly, he said, "Come over for Christmas tomorrow."

Margorie was initially taken aback. "You don't want me at your house," she insisted. "It's family time. And you just met me!"

"On the contrary, Margorie Tomlinson, I want you there," Daniel assured her. "My daughter and sister won't stop pestering me about this 'new woman in my life.'"

Margorie's cheeks burned with a mix of pleasure and embarrassment. Did she really have it in her to attend a family Christmas?

"Come on," Daniel said. "Tell me you have something better to do."

"I planned to organize my sock drawer," Margorie joked.

"Oh. Well, in that case, you should stay home." Daniel's face was stoic. "I know how important your sock drawer is to you."

Margorie gasped with laughter. "Daniel! I just don't know what to say."

"Say you'll come over and eat a ridiculously enormous Christmas feast with my family and me," Daniel said. "Say you'll let me give you your present by my Christmas tree. Say you'll stick around a little while in my life before fleeing back to wherever you came from."

This last sentence tugged at Margorie's heartstrings. For a long time, she gazed at him, her thoughts swirling through potentialities. Yes – she could flee Martha's Vineyard whenever she wanted to, return to Wilmington, to the life Tom had left her alone in. But what good would that do? Daniel was offering her something here. And before Estelle had left yesterday morning, she'd squeezed Margorie's hand and said, "Don't be a stranger. I'm sure Roland would love to see you, too."

Margorie dropped her chin into a nod. There was

nothing else in the world she'd rather do than spend Christmas with Daniel. She was the luckiest woman in the world.

* * *

After she rang the bell at Daniel's place, Margorie adjusted a pumpkin pie in her arms and waited, her heart performing backflips across her diaphragm. A split-second later came the squeal of a toddler, followed by the quick bounces of his little feet. Then, his face appeared in the doorway, all cheeks and a few little teeth poking out between his smile. It had been ages since Margorie had spent time with children. The sight of Daniel's grandson, wild with the magic of Christmas, thrilled her.

"Welcome! Merry Christmas!" Daniel drew her into an embrace as Aiden babbled happily beneath them, asking question after question about this stranger.

"Aiden," Daniel said gently as he lifted him into his arms, "this is my dear friend, Margorie. And Margorie, this is my grandson, Aiden."

"It's a pleasure to meet you," Margorie said. "Merry Christmas."

Aiden hid his face in Daniel's shoulder, peeking back only slightly to continue to inspect the new guest. Margorie and Daniel laughed.

"He's just like me," Margorie offered. "It takes me a little while to warm up."

A moment later, a young woman in her twenties and a man of a similar age entered the foyer. The woman was introduced as Caitlin, Daniel's daughter, and the man was Dean, her husband. Caitlin collected her son from

Daniel and beamed at Margorie, endlessly curious about her. It wasn't every day you met your father's new girl-friend, Margorie knew. She also knew that Daniel's ex had been the one to end things. All Caitlin wanted was for her father to find happiness again.

"Come in! Come in!" Daniel ushered everyone deeper into the house, where his sister, Lisa, and his mother watched a Christmas episode of *The Golden Girls*.

"Oh, I love this show," Margorie said, smiling at Daniel's mother, who suffered from dementia and hardly glanced up.

"It's on all the time around here," Lisa said as she shook Margorie's hand. "Mom always wants to watch it."

"You must have great taste," Margorie said to Daniel's mother, who hardly glanced her way.

Daniel seemed unbothered by his mother's illness just then. Probably, he was just used to it. He disappeared into the kitchen for a moment and returned with a Christmas cookie shaped like a reindeer and slathered with an inch's worth of frosting at the least.

"My goodness!" Margorie exclaimed.

"Mommy and me made them," Aiden announced from below, speaking to Margorie for the first time.

Margorie took a bite, filling her mouth with sharp sugar and dough. "Mmm," she said loudly. "Aiden, you are really talented! Have you baked before?"

Aiden shook his head, his eyes glinting. He was pleased.

Not long after Margorie arrived, they sat down for dinner. Daniel, Caitlin, and Lisa had slaved over a feast—turkey, stuffing, mashed potatoes with gravy, macaroni and cheese for Aiden, and garlic green beans. Margorie sat comfortably between Daniel and his sister, Lisa, who reported she was heading into the city tomorrow to meet her daughter.

"Margorie goes to New York all the time," Daniel said proudly.

"Not all the time," Margorie said. "But I've had a few book launches there, yes. The publisher sometimes puts me up in hotels I wouldn't have even been able to imagine as a kid."

Caitlin smiled as she spooned more macaroni and cheese onto Aiden's plate. "I hope this doesn't embarrass you, but I read one of your books. *A Christmas Dream?*"

Margorie dropped her chin with acknowledgment. "That was the last one I wrote."

Caitlin's eyes widened. "I spent all evening the other night totally lost in that world! When it was over, I cried to Dean about it for hours."

Dean laughed. "She really did. I'm not a romance guy, myself, but I started reading it, too."

"He is a romance guy," Caitlin teased. "You should have heard some of the stuff he told me when we were first dating. It was like he'd walked straight out of a romance novel."

"Maybe I did walk straight out of a romance novel," Dean said. "Why not? Stranger things have happened."

Caitlin rolled her eyes and laughed. "Your daddy is crazy," she told Aiden, then kissed the top of his head.

"Are you working on anything right now?" Lisa asked. She didn't seem the type to read romance novels, which was okay.

"I am, actually."

Daniel's eyes widened. Margorie had surprised him and herself with this admittance.

"Yesterday morning, I got lost in new notes for a story idea," Margorie admitted. "I've already written the first chapter."

Caitlin clapped her hands. "That's exciting!"

"What is it about?" Dean asked.

Caitlin swatted him. "You don't just ask someone that. She has a process, obviously. She won't share that with us."

"It's okay!" Margorie smiled wider and took another helping of green beans. "All I can tell you right now is this. It's about second chances. It's about being seventy years old and still finding new ways to dream about the future." She glanced at Daniel, whose eyes were heavy with emotion. Was that love lurking behind them? She couldn't be sure. She had to wait and see.

"I'll read it as soon as it comes out," Caitlin announced.

"We all will," Lisa affirmed.

The rest of the dinner flowed easily. Margorie asked everyone questions about themselves, about their work, and about Caitlin and Dean's recent move from California. Aiden frequently interrupted with funny anecdotes about something called "the macaroni and cheese monster," his friends at preschool, and his grandmother back in California. This was Daniel's ex. Margorie expected the air to shift with nerves after this mention, but nobody seemed to mind. "Yes, we're going to see Grandma next week, aren't we?" Caitlin said. "We're going to fly in an airplane again!" At this, Aiden clapped.

Between dinner and pie, Margorie excused herself to Daniel's office, where she sat between stacks of books and notepads, scribbled with grocery lists and meditations on his life. Although she tried to avoid looking at them, she did manage to read one that said: "Keep going. Things are about to get better. I just know it."

The phone rang out across the Nantucket Sound, four, five, then six rings before Estelle answered it with an air of surprise.

"Merry Christmas!"

Margorie was surprised at how pleased she was to hear Estelle's voice again. She'd begun to think of her as a kindred spirit, a sister she'd never been allowed to have.

"Merry Christmas," Margorie said, suddenly nervous. "I hope you and your family are doing well?"

"We just opened too many presents," Estelle said, "and now I'm about to eat my third cookie of the day. Nobody has reminded me of my seventy-year-old metabolism, so I'm going to ignore it today."

"Good idea," Margorie said with a laugh. She rolled Daniel's office chair forward and planted her elbows on his desk, listening to the soft laughter coming from Estelle's house. "I just wanted to thank you again for coming over the other night. I don't know how to tell you this, but it was probably one of the best nights of my life."

Estelle was quiet for a moment. Margorie was suddenly terrified she would tell Margorie never to contact her again, to tell her that now that their feud was over, their communication would be, too.

But then, Estelle said, "I feel like we were always meant to be friends, Margorie."

Margorie laughed with relief. "I feel the same way."

When Margorie returned to Daniel's living room, she dropped onto the couch beside him and allowed herself to be swallowed in a hug. On the floor, Aiden and Caitlin played with his new train set as Lisa and their mother put on another *Golden Girls* episode, ready to ease into a lazy afternoon by the fire. Margorie couldn't remember feeling half this happy in the past five years.

And, within the year, she knew she would finish her next book. She couldn't wait.

Chapter Twenty-Four

On the morning Estelle had returned from Margorie's beach house, she'd placed the manuscript "What Should Have Been" on the counter next to Roland as he poured himself a mug of coffee. He immediately set the pot of coffee back and stared at the stack of papers as though it was made of gold. "Is that what I think it is?" he whispered finally, lifting his eyes toward Estelle's.

For a long time, Estelle and Roland sat in the sunroom with the manuscript on the coffee table and sunlight pouring through the floor-to-ceiling windows. Luscious green plants surrounded them, and the air felt nourishing. Christmas music sprinkled through the speakers.

"I can't believe she's had it all this time," Roland said finally.

"Neither can I." Estelle rubbed her temples. "She told me she eventually regretted taking it and then promptly forgot about it. But she couldn't bring herself to ever throw it away."

Roland shook his head. "I can't help but think about

myself as that young, eighteen-year-old. I had no idea what I was putting her through."

Estelle dropped her head on his chest and listened to the thudding of his heart. "She told me more about her husband, Tom, last night. About the wonderful life they had before his accident. About how sometimes, she wondered if anyone in the world had ever loved anyone as much as she loved him."

Roland stroked Estelle's hair and remained silent.

"She said that when she fell in love with Tom, she fully understood why you had to leave the University of Massachusetts," Estelle went on. "She saw into your mind in that moment. And she was so happy for you."

Roland sniffed. Estelle wondered if he was on the verge of tears.

"I told her about our children," Estelle went on. "About Samantha's social work. About how handsome and moral and good Charlie is. About Hilary's interior design and recent eye surgery." She shook her head. "I could have talked to Margorie all night long, I think. When we finally went to bed, it was three. I felt the way I did as a much younger girl, sleeping over at a friend's place. We couldn't shut up."

* * *

Christmas Day at Estelle and Roland's place was chaos. Food ladened every countertop and every table, and wine glasses, beer bottles, and glasses of juice appeared on every surface. Estelle whipped in and out of the kitchen, preparing dinner, delivering Christmas cookies to grandchildren, and pausing frequently for a spot of gossip and a sip of her wine. In the minutes after her phone call with

Margorie, she shivered with adrenaline, so much so that Hilary and Samantha sequestered her in the kitchen and demanded what was wrong.

This was when Estelle pulled out the manuscript to show her daughters. Samantha and Hilary handled the old notebook pages as though they were an ancient scroll from Egypt. Hilary immediately wept on the first page.

"Let me get this straight," Samantha demanded. "You wrote this when you thought everything was over between you and Dad?"

Estelle nodded. "Your grandmother was very sick, and I was extremely lonely. Your Great Aunt Jessabelle suggested I start writing here and there. At first, I refused the idea. I think I was too depressed. Your grandfather had just left, and I was up to my ears in work."

Hilary and Samantha's eyes widened. Estelle wasn't entirely sure she'd shared with them the specifics of this time of her life yet.

"That's in *A Bright Christmas*!" Hilary pointed out. "I thought maybe bits and pieces of it were fictionalized!"

"No," Estelle said with a laugh. "Most of that book really happened to me. I just wish I could go back and edit it now. There's so much to say, now, about Margorie's involvement in that time period."

"What about a sequel?" Samantha suggested, taking a Christmas cookie from a platter and nibbling at the edges.

"It's not a bad idea," Estelle said.

Hilary crossed her arms. "Now that Margorie has released a statement about these accusations, has the publisher reached out to you? Have they put together a new offer?"

"They better have," Samantha grumbled.

"They sent me an apology email," Estelle said. "And asked if we could meet in New York in January to go over a new contract."

"You had better ask for way more money this time!" Hilary cried.

"You're a mega-celebrity after this feud," Samantha agreed.

"Margorie and I talked about that, too," Estelle went on. "About how our careers have skyrocketed after this intense internet hashtag nonsense. We discussed having a fake feud in a few years just in case we need to get our sales up there." She winked.

"Mom!" Samantha and Hilary cried in unison before bursting into laughter.

"Margorie sounds like a card," Hilary said.

"I don't trust her," Samantha said.

"You can't trust everyone," Estelle agreed. "But we're sniffing each other out right now. And I have a hunch we'll be fast friends."

"You're too forgiving, Mom," Samantha suggested.

Estelle raised her shoulders. "What else is there but forgiveness? I think it's the single greatest thing we, as humans, can do."

Hilary and Samantha gave one another knowing glances. For decades, they'd squabbled with one another, bent on proving they were right and the other was wrong. Yet they, too, had learned the power of forgiveness in recent months. They'd since built a powerful friendship, one Estelle couldn't fully comprehend.

A moment later, Roland appeared in the doorway, a dominant shadow carrying a small bottle of beer. He looked tired and red-cheeked after his hours of conversation and laughter with his children and grandchildren.

That, and eating – so much eating. Estelle imagined they would sleep very late tomorrow, perhaps rising around ten for coffee and leftover Christmas cookies. She couldn't wait to sit quietly with him in the sunroom and watch the snow.

Ultimately, all of this – Samantha and Hilary, the grandchildren cackling in the side room, Charlie and his son on the back porch for a breath of fresh air, Chuck Coleman telling stories to Sheila, Marcy with her boyfriend, Jax – had happened because Estelle and Roland had fallen in love, once upon a time. The Coleman Family wouldn't have been as messy and beautiful and complicated and joyous without Estelle and Roland taking that first step at the age of fourteen.

"Do you ever think how strange all this is?" Estelle asked Roland quietly after Hilary and Samantha left the kitchen to chat with their girls in the dining room.

"Almost every day," Roland admitted. "I have to pinch myself."

Estelle pressed her ear against his chest, and Roland wrapped his strong arms around her. They gazed out the kitchen window, listening to the shuddering laughter of so many family members peppered around their house. A bright red cardinal landed on the tree branch by the window and twitched his head to peer at them, probably just as curious about them as they were about him.

"Thank you for doing life with me," Estelle whispered.

"Are you talking to that bird?"

Estelle swatted Roland and drew her head back to gaze into his eyes. "You'll never change, will you?"

"Never," Roland promised. "I know you won't, either."

"I love you to bits, Roland Coleman. Don't you ever forget it."

"I won't," Roland said. "I'm the hero in every single one of your romance novels. All of your fans know how handsome, dashing, and wonderful I am."

Estelle swatted him again as he bent her into a kiss, there in the silence of their kitchen. She felt eighteen years old again; it was the very same love, the very same emotion she had the day he'd come to her doorstep, his suitcase behind him, sweat on his brow. He'd said: "I've quit college. I'm never going back. Be my bride." She hadn't hesitated. She'd fallen into his arms. And their lives followed.

Coming Next in the Coleman Series

Pre Order Winter Sun

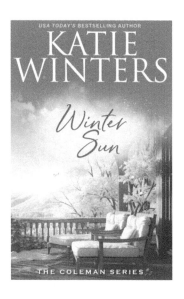

Other Books by Katie Winters

The Vineyard Sunset Series

Secrets of Mackinac Island Series

Sisters of Edgartown Series

A Katama Bay Series

A Mount Desert Island Series

A Nantucket Sunset Series

Connect with Katie Winters

Amazon
BookBub
Facebook
Newsletter

To receive exclusive updates from Katie Winters please
sign up to be on her Newsletter!
CLICK HERE TO SUBSCRIBE

Made in United States
Cleveland, OH
08 July 2025

18350751R00118